Westinghouse Radio Tube.
Photo by Gilles Messier, 2012.

petrabooks.ca

"Technology…is not mere set-dressing in the grand drama of humanity. It is humanity—its very soul and essence."

— from the Author's preface.

Mid-century speculative fiction

… … …

Left: A German sentry stands guard in Kiev, Ukraine in 1941.
theatlantic.com/infocus/2011/07/world-war-ii-operation-barbarossa/100112/

Centre: Hand and Atom advertisement, c.1950s
ultraswank.net/science/our-friend-the-atom—-part-1

Right: Russian cosmonaut Aleksey Leonov performing the first spacewalk during the Voskhod II mission, March 18, 1965.
mostlyodd.com/voskhod-2-the-cursed-peak-of-soviet-space/

The Second World War. Nuclear Power. Space Exploration. Three powerful forces that forever changed the course of history. In these nine new stories Gilles Messier explores our intimate and often fickle relationship with science and technology in the 1940s, 1950s and 1960s, and how it came to define our past, present and future.

Self-portrait by Gilles Messier, 2010

Gilles Messier was born in Winnipeg in 1989 and studies aerospace engineering at Carleton University, Ottawa. As well as writing, he designs and develops mechanical devices and innovations, and enjoys painting inter-war period travel posters, and studying history and philosophy.

BEST BEFORE DEC 31 1969

**Our
Own
Devices**

… … …

**By
Gilles
Messier**

… … …

With 27 photographs

from the archives

of science and technology

Petra Books

petrabooks.ca

Control room of Battersea Power Station, London, July 1933. (left detail)
nickelinthemachine.com/2009/05/the-cathedral-of-electrons-in-battersea/

... ...

The story of civilization is, in a sense, the story of engineering—that long and arduous struggle to make the forces of nature work for man's good.

—Sprague de Camp

The measure of a civilization is how much you take for granted.

—Louis Dudek

There is nothing in machinery, there is nothing in embankments and railways and iron bridges and engineering devices to oblige them to be ugly. Ugliness is the measure of imperfection.

—H.G. Wells

Associated Press correspondent Alvin Steinkopf, reporting the tense political situation in Danzig, Poland, July 11, 1939
theatlantic.com /infocus/2011/06/world-war-ii-the-invasion-of-poland-and-the-winter-war/100094/

... ...

For Roberta, who saw the writer in me.

Turbine hall at Calder Hall, England, circa 1956
wodumedia.com/sellafield-nuclear-power-station/the-boiler-house-of-the-calder-hall-nuclear-power-plant-where-heat-is-converted-into-high-pressure-steam-in-order-to-power-turbines/

Contents

Control panel, La Chaudière Hydroelectric Power Station, Ottawa Canada Photo by Gilles Messier, June 4, 2011

About This Book

THE 20TH CENTURY saw the most dramatic changes in technology and society than any other period in history, particularly during the 30 years between the 1940 and 1970. This book collects the volumes A Fresh Invasion of Savages, A is for Atom, and Leaving the Cradle which encompass my literary thoughts on three pivotal events that defined these decades: the Second World War, the development of nuclear power, and the exploration of space, respectively. Through these stories I have attempted to capture the zeitgeist of the mid-20th century and explore, from various perspectives, its impact upon our past, present and future.

—GM

Preface: On Literary Materialism

A COLLEAGUE OF MINE, upon reading my story Hypothermia, asked: "Why the excessive technical and historical detail? How does it serve the story or characters? What's the point?" Thankfully, his opinion of my oeuvre's literary merit has proven to be the exception rather than the rule. Nonetheless, this incident made me closely examine my writing style and define the general philosophy underpinning my work—which, for lack of a better term, I shall dub Literary Materialism.

From an early age I have been fascinated by machines, aircraft and space travel—concrete, technical topics. History has also been a favorite subject—the history of warfare in general and the history of weaponry in particular. It should thus come as no surprise that my inspiration to become an author came not from 'respectable' literature—Dickens, Carroll or Louis- Stevenson—but from the techno-thrillers of Michael Crichton (Jurassic Park, The Andromeda Strain). What drew me to Crichton were not his characters, themes or symbolism, but his incredible ability to spin scientific and technical fact into plausible thrilling scenarios. Here was an author who seemed to write for me alone, giving me exactly what I wanted. My first attempt at literature, a techno-thriller titled Vostok, greatly aped Crichton's style - and was an amateurish, clichéd mess. Though my writing style gradually matured, I remained fascinated with technology and with reconciling its place in literature. Eventually I came to the realization that technology—from the simplest clay pot to the computer—is not mere set-dressing in the grand drama of humanity. It is humanity—its very soul and essence. And while writers for thousands of years have scrutinized mankind from every conceivable angle—its hopes and dreams, its triumphs and tragedies, its heroes and villains—one perspective remains largely untapped: to examine humanity through its stuff.

Our current species might be Homo Sapiens ('Thinking Man'), but one of our earliest hominid ancestors was more aptly named Homo Habilis, variously translated as 'Able Man', 'Handy Man', or 'Man the Toolmaker'. In paleontology, one can glean much from the bones of an organism: where it lived; how fast it ran, swam, or flew; what it ate. But such techniques work only on creatures whose lives and abilities—their entire being—are encompassed by their flesh and blood. On its own, a human skeleton reveals surprisingly little: that we walk upright, that we are omnivores, and that our brain cavities are larger than in most mammals—hardly a comprehensive portrait of humanity. To truly know humans, one must look at their 'stuff'—the objects they create and use every day. Objects define us. Without objects, we could not survive. We have no insulating fur, no sharp teeth or claws. We cannot fly, nor run, jump, swim or climb quickly. All necessities we must craft with our minds. Stuff makes our lives possible, and when we are all dead and our bones rotted away, only stuff will remain to mark our existence. In his 1982 book The Extended Phenotype, naturalist Richard Dawkins argues that the products of behavior—from termite mounds to beaver dams—are as much a product of an organism's DNA as the shape of its body. On its own, a termite is a rather ordinary-looking insect. But inside its multi-spired mound, with all its intricate, sophisticated passageways and ventilation shafts, it becomes something extraordinary. So too with humans, though our creations are unfettered by rigid genetic programming. There is no limit to the spires we can raise.

While it is commonly believed that society is shaped and advanced by philosophers and other progenitors of so-called higher ideas, in fact the wheels of history are largely turned by the unseen corps of practical builders who craft our technology. Indeed, our modern metaphysics and other advanced ideas owe their very existence to the development of agriculture and food surpluses, which allowed specialization in crafts other than farming. Our modern, ultra-productive way of life, tightly-scheduled and networked, was inconceivable before accurate clocks allowed us to divide up our lives, and electric lights turned night into day. And if waiting weeks to communicate by letter, writing a paper by hand or typewriter, playing telephone tag via landline and pager, using a paper map, or waiting for photographic film to develop seem quaint—despite being common tasks until fairly recently—it is because society is thoroughly defined by its technology. So integral is modern technology to the fabric of our lives that we struggle to imagine how previous generations functioned without it.

Technology is also a greater force for social change than many care to admit. By allowing ordinary people to more easily arm themselves, the cheap and reliable AK-47 did more to fuel the explosion of 20th-century revolutions than political ideology or ethnic tensions (which had existed since long before). And by giving women direct control over their bodies, the birth control pill did more for women's rights than any liberation movement. It is this intimate relationship between humans and technology that fascinates me. In my story The Luddite (not featured in this collection), a psychiatrist struggles to treat a patient who believes machines are taking over the world. Meanwhile, she obliviously submits to the seemingly innocuous devices—telephones, pagers, parking meters —that dictate the frantic pace of her life. These devices are deliberately placed front and centre, but are so commonplace to the reader that they melt into the background, preserving the story's subtext.

All this brings me back to Hypothermia. Conventional writing wisdom dictates that descriptive detail of objects should only be used to set the scene or establish essential plot points; anything more is indulgent and distracts from the story and characters. This supposedly common-sense argument, however, ignores the power of Literary Materialism—

viewing the world through the lens of inanimate objects. Hypothermia centers around the true story of Nazi Doctor Sigmund Rascher, who, in 1943 at Dachau Concentration Camp, studied the effects of hypothermia by freezing live subjects in baths of ice water. In writing this story I extensively researched these experiments, striving to depict them as accurately as possible. This choice was not merely a didactic one, for what truly disturbed me about Rascher's work was precisely his meticulousness. Unlike Dr. Josef Mengele at Auschwitz, whose sadistic experiments were largely haphazard and unstructured, Rascher conducted his research with the utmost scientific rigor—so much so, in fact, that his data is still considered valid today. He strictly controlled every aspect of the experiments, leaving nothing to chance. The horror, then, comes from what was overlooked. In the midst of their meticulous preparations and procedures, Rascher and his colleagues seemed to ignore a simple truth: that human beings were being frozen alive against their will. Through such chilling detachment and obfuscating attention to detail, I sought to capture what German philosopher Hannah Arendt once called the 'Banality of Evil'. The Devil was truly in the details

Perhaps the most common piece of advice given to budding authors is 'show, don't tell'. No concept better underscores the utility of Literary Materialism. Sherlock Holmes, in his various incarnations, was notorious for his so-called 'Sherlock Scans'—'cold readings' in which he could deduce a subject's entire personality and life story simply from their external appearance and possessions. These characters needn't speak a single line; their entire beings were laid out plainly for all to see. Our objects—the clothes we wear, the cars we drive, the food we buy—define us more honestly than we care to admit. Objects do not lie. They reveal our innermost desires—to fit in, to stand out, to provoke, to disappear, to be loved, to be feared, to be respected—more poignantly than words. In Stephen Leacock's 1910 story Number Fifty-Six, Chinese launderer Ah-Yen wistfully reminisces about the titular former customer, whose entire life story he infers from the state of his laundry. Through exam notes scrawled on cuffs, fluctuating ratios of linen and silk handkerchiefs, broken buttons and a final bloodstained shirt, Ah-Yen traces #56's journey through university, graduation, first love, romantic strife, depression and apparent suicide (revealed by the narrator, the real #56, as merely a cigarette burn and red ink stain). This oblique approach serves to make #56 more mysterious and intriguing, and capture Ah-Yen's hopelessly romantic imagination, than would be possible through a conventional narrative. Even in real life, our possessions speak when we cannot. In 1985, the public's long fascination with the Titanic was renewed when oceanographer Robert Ballard discovered the wreck at the bottom of the Atlantic. Ballard and future explorers found thousands of artifacts littering the wreck site, but no human remains; they had vanished, long ago consumed by bacteria. But one photograph hauntingly captured the humanity and tragedy of the disaster—the white porcelain face of a child's doll, lying half-buried on the sea floor. All that remains of a young life, long ago faded into the abyss. There can be no better memorial.

Literary Materialism serves to break down a great barrier separating literature from another great art form—the film. As an art of images, film is an ideal medium for subtlety and visual symbolism. Important objects and symbols can be hidden in plain sight, and a character's fleeting expression or silent action can speak volumes. In literature, a medium of words, it is difficult to show and not tell, for every element of the story—setting, characters' appearance, action, dialogue, inner thoughts and motivations—must be explicitly spelled out. By approaching the world through objects, however, one can subtly and profoundly reach deep truths about humanity. Thoughts and words can be fleeting and superficial, but even the simplest objects require time and effort to produce. What we choose to build speaks to our deepest desires and priorities. A cheap, fragile plastic toy may seem simple, but it requires an extraordinary amount of talent, effort and resources to create the design, machine the moulds, tool the factory, and mass produce and distribute the toys. Why, then, do we build such baubles? Why did Neolithic people build Stonehenge, or the Easter Islanders raise great stone heads, or the Nazca Indians carve monumental tableaux into hillsides? Like the shadows in Plato's Cave, the objects of humanity hint at deeper truths, tantalizingly hidden just out of view. Such is the essence of effective literature: to make us think and feel, but not reveal too much. Thus it is through objects that I have chosen to tell many of the stories in this book: the titular monolith in The Girl at Panel 857, the makeshift laboratory in The Fisherman and the Genie, the spacecraft in In the Ocean of Storms.

These tales present a different take on humanity, the engineer's view: that we are what we make.

—Gilles Messier

British Troops Charging in North Africa, November 27, 1942.
theatlantic.com/infocus/2011/09/world-war-ii-the-north-african-campaign/100140/

Part I

A

Fresh

Invasion

Of

Savages

German Afrika Korps tank crewman in Libya, April 14, 1941
theatlantic.com/infocus/2011/07/world-war-ii-conflict-spreads-around-the-globe/100107/

... ...

What is History, after all? History is the facts which become legends in the end. Legends are lies which become history in the end.

—Jean Cocteau

Mortal danger is an effective antidote for fixed ideas.

—Erwin Rommel

Every generation is a fresh invasion of savages.

—William Hervey Allen

VE-Day celebration in Toronto, May 8, 1945
toronto.ca/archives/ve1.htm

Foreword: The 'Good' War

IN THIS DAY AND AGE, it is difficult to admit to believing in myths. The very word conjures up images of the Greek pantheon and other ancient tales. Myths, however, are merely stories with which we explain our origins and define our cultural identity. And while it is true that religions still flourish today, these are largely ancient myths that have survived to the present day. Modern, freshly-minted myths are often more subtle and difficult to pin down.

Of all human activities, none is as prolific a source of myths as warfare. Literature abounds with tales of great warriors and their exploits on the battlefield, inflated and embellished through countless retellings to the point of legend. And while we, with our modern record-keeping, may believe we have a clear, accurate view of history, the troubadour tradition of legend-making nonetheless persists. For evidence, one need only examine one of the most pivotal events of the Twentieth Century: the Second World War. Though a relatively recent conflict, WWII is nonetheless shrouded in countless myths and misconceptions. Perhaps most persistent is the idea that D-Day was the turning point of the war in Europe. In reality, the Third Reich's downfall began a full year prior at the 1943 Battle of Kursk, when the Red Army finally pushed the Germans into permanent retreat towards Berlin. Had the Western Allies never landed in Normandy, the Soviet Union would likely have defeated Germany single-handedly. Post-war Europe would have been considerably different.

Myths surrounding WWII can turn up in the most unexpected places. Consider the event that started the war: Germany's invasion of Poland in September 1939. While few deny the unprovoked and belligerent nature of the attack, many perceive the invasion as having been a fairly conventional military operation. Yet even at this early stage of the war, Nazi atrocities were well underway. Following behind the advancing Panzers, roving Einsatzgruppen death squads rounded up and executed Jews, Polish intelligentsia and other 'undesirables'. The cities of Warsaw and Weilun, of negligible military importance, were mercilessly bombed by the Luftwaffe. And just prior to the invasion, German commandos in Polish uniforms carried out staged attacks against German border posts, allowing Hitler to justify his invasion as retaliation against Polish aggression. While the invasion of Poland was many things, it was far from 'conventional'.

Far more overlooked are atrocities perpetrated by the Allies. With the exception of Hiroshima and Nagasaki, few such incidents have stuck in the popular consciousness. Yet for a year before the atomic bombings, the US Air Force leveled Tokyo and other Japanese cities in a series of devastating firebombing operations. On March 9, 1945, Operation Meetinghouse, the deadliest air raid in history, killed 100,000 people in a single night. In Europe, the Royal Air Force launched a series of firebombing raids—codenamed Operation Gomorrah—against Hamburg and Dresden, sparking ferocious firestorms that killed tens of thousands of civilians. Dresden in particular was of little military importance, leading some to condemn the Gomorrah raids as terror bombings to demoralize the civilian populace. The war also saw instances of Allied troops executing unarmed prisoners and even civilians. In the Pacific, it was common for U.S. soldiers to defile Japanese corpses, even keeping body parts as souvenirs. Indeed, 60% of Japanese bodies repatriated from the Mariana islands were missing their skulls. Though certain incidents led to court-martial, no equivalent to the Nuremberg Trials was ever held for Allied personnel.

Consider further the following question: which two nations tested chemical and biological weapons on human subjects during WWII? The answer is Japan and Canada. In 1942, at the Suffield Research Station in Alberta, volunteer troops were made to stand in a field wearing only standard uniforms and gas masks while an aircraft sprayed them with mustard gas. They were then marched back to base, where the burns inflicted by the gas were studied. Meanwhile, laboratories in Montreal weaponized diseases such as Psittacosis, Tularemia and Rocky Mountain Spotted Fever, and Anthrax was grown on Grosse Isle, a former quarantine station in the St. Lawrence. The Japanese research program has also largely been forgotten, despite barbarity surpassing that of the Nazis. The Japanese Army's Unit 731 tested biological and chemical weapons on Chinese civilians, often dissecting subjects alive without anesthetic. Nonetheless, few Unit 731 researchers were tried for war crimes; most were quietly pardoned and integrated into American weapons programs.

Thus the greatest myth of WWII is that it was the 'last good war,' the last justified, unambiguous clash between an absolute good and absolute evil. As with all of history, the truth is far more complex. Close examination of the conflict reveals heroes and villains on both sides and moral ambiguity all around. There is more to WWII than the Time-Life photographs etched in our collective consciousness.

The Second World War has always been a particular fascination of mine. In the course of my research I have uncovered countless obscure and strange anecdotes, from daring raids and forgotten battle plans to bizarre secret weapons and strange twists of fate—so many, in fact, that it is sometimes hard to believe so much occurred in the span of only six years. Such is always the case with history: the deeper one digs, the more astonishing details and connections appear, like the multiplying heads of the mythical Hydra. These obscure facets of war inspire the stories collected in this volume. They reveal the hidden war, the forgotten war. It is my hope that these stories will inspire the reader to think differently about WWII, to re-evaluate their perception of history, and uncover their own personal myths.

··· ··· ···

We knew the world would not be the same. A few people laughed.
A few people cried. Most people were silent. I remembered the line from the Hindu Scripture, the Baghavad Gita. Vishnu
is trying to persuade the Prince that he should do his duty, and to impress him takes on his multi-armed form and says,
'Now I am become Death, the Destroyer of Worlds'. I suppose we all thought that, one way or another.

—J. Robert Oppenheimer

Calutron Operators at the Beta-2 uranium separation facility control room, Oak Ridge, Tennessee, 1945
en.wikipedia.org/ wiki/File:Y12_Calutron_Operators.jpg

The Girl at Panel 857

Oak Ridge, Tennessee
January 5, 1945

MAJOR WINTERS marched briskly down the narrow halls, his polished boots clicking a sharp cadence on the shiny green linoleum. Vera, in her restricting pencil skirt, could barely keep up. Her pumps slid precariously on the newly-buffed surface.

"Keep up," said Major Winters flatly. "Eyes forward."

Vera nodded meekly and snapped her wandering eyes forward. She couldn't help herself: the temptation was too great. Already she had caught glimpses of strange and mysterious things: huge machines bristling with wires and dials, laboratories bustling with white-coated scientists, chalkboards filled with arcane equations. The whole building was abuzz with frantic activity, the nature of which was a mystery. Whatever it was, it must have been important. From every wall, posters urgently exclaimed: the walls have ears.

Vera fixed her eyes on the back of Major Winters' head. He was a fine-looking man, she thought, the young ambitious type, the kind who'd get any girl he wanted. But he acted like Vera was some stray dog or tag-along child: a necessary nuisance. She couldn't tell if he was just playing up his military discipline or if he really was one of those careerist, married-to-the-Army types.

The hallway grew darker as they passed deeper into the complex. There were no windows here. The walls were bare concrete, the doors solid slabs of metal. Above each door glowed a red or green bulb, like oversized Christmas lights. The hall smelled of wet concrete and fresh paint, as if the whole structure had been raised overnight.

"Through here", grunted Winters, holding open a door. Vera scurried through under his irritated gaze.

Vera drew a small gasp as she entered a vast hall lined with row upon row of tall battleship-grey control panels. The monolithic devices, stretching from floor to ceiling, seemed to extend forever into the distance, like one of those funhouse mirrors at the fair. A bevy of young women her age sat on wooden stools before the panels, silently monitoring and adjusting various knobs and switches. A man with a clipboard patrolled the hall, pausing occasionally to adjust a dial. He strode towards Vera and Major Winters as they entered.

"New one for me, Major?" he said.

Winters nodded.

"How do…" Vera started, extending her hand.

"You'll be at Panel 857", interrupted the man with the clipboard. He pointed to nearby vacant panel. "Sit down."

Vera nodded nervously and sat, resting her hands demurely on her lap as she faced the bewildering array of gauges and knobs.

"I"m Dr. Riley," he said. "Floor supervisor for Beta 2."

Not wasting a second, Dr. Riley launched into rapid-fire instructions, his finger flying over the panel in quick jerks.

"See these two gauges here? You'll need to maintain those between 44.95 and 45.05. Top gain is that knob here, bottom gain that one there. That selector switch there toggles between coarse and fine adjust. On fine adjust the reading should be maintained between 44.955 and 45.005. Now, when you adjust these, your voltage reading on that gauge there is going to wander, so you'll want to optimize…"

"I'm sorry, Sir, er—Doctor," Vera interrupted. "But… what does this machine do?"

Dr. Riley hesitated.

"That's a matter of national security," interjected Major Winters, still hovering behind them. "Now you'll refrain from asking any more questions pertaining to this assignment, other than those relevant to carrying out your duties. Is that understood?"

Vera nodded meekly, eyes wide.

"Thank you Major," said Riley. "I'll handle things from here."

Winters gave a short, curt nod and turned on his heel. He paused before departing, glancing over his shoulder at Vera.

"You're doing a great service for your country, ma'am."

Nashville
April 11, 1961

From the powder room, Vera heard the metallic click and hiss of the television being switched on. The faint audio quickly grew loud enough to hear.

"…began today in Jerusalem. Eichmann, director of transportation for Hitler's 'Final Solution' is accused of arranging the deportation and extermination of some six million Jews during the war. Having fled Europe for South America,

Eichmann was captured last year in Buenos Aires by Israeli Intelligence so he may stand trial before the very people he once attempted to exterminate. Here Eichmann arrives in the courtroom, shielded behind bulletproof glass to prevent any administration of vigilante justice. The judges at this tribunal are…"

"Honey," Vera called as she trotted down the stairs. "You're going to be late for work."

"I have a few minutes," mumbled Charlie from behind his newspaper. "Chief Engineer is usually a half hour late anyway."

"Well, then I'll be late," said Vera, pushing down the paper.

Charlie grunted and raised the paper anew. "Alright, let me finish this article. Then we'll go."

"Good," said Vera, pulling her coat off the hook by the door.

"Huh, you believe this guy?" scoffed Charlie, pointing to the television. "Says he was 'only following orders'. Goddamn Nazis…"

"What? You never followed orders in the Air Force?" said Vera absently, searching for her keys.

"Yeah, but they never ordered us to murder six million innocent people."

"Maybe he didn't know what he was doing. Like they said: he arranged transportations…"

"Yeah," said Charlie. " 'cause an innocent man runs and hides in South America…"

He suddenly lowered his paper, staring incredulously at Vera. "Are you seriously vouching for this Nazi?"

"No, of course not," said Vera, picking up her handbag. "I'm just playing Devil's Advocate. That's what scientists do, don't they?"

Charlie smirked.

"But seriously," she continued. "They never gave orders you didn't like or understand?"

Charlie tossed his paper aside and rose from the sofa. "Difference is: we always knew we were doing the right thing," he said, putting on his coat. "And what do you know about it anyway? You weren't there. How many moral choices did you make working in some stateside factory?"

Vera did not answer. She was silent for many long moments, staring at the neat row of framed photographs by the door. Charlie, dapper in his crisp uniform, standing under the engine of his B-29 bomber. Vera smiling proudly in gown and mortarboard, diploma in hand. The both of them standing at the altar.

She sighed. "Yes…you're right. I hope he hangs."

Charlie pecked her on the cheek. "Don't want to be late."

Oak Ridge
February 16, 1945

Vera glanced again at the overhead clock, making sure that Dr. Riley was out of sight. She had been reprimanded before for not keeping her eyes on her work. There was little left to do, though, but watch the clock. A month ago, reining in the restlessly jumping and drifting dials had been an exercise in vigilance and concentration; eight-hour shifts would fly past. Now, Vera could swiftly and automatically correct the most abrupt, unexpected twitch within seconds. She played her panel like a musical instrument and kept it singing contentedly all day. Once-frantic shifts were now calm eternities.

At long last the clock read eight o'clock.

"SHIFT CHANGE!" said Dr. Riley.

As the night shift filed in, Vera made final adjustments to her panel. It was then that she noticed something strange. Panel 855 was always operated at night by her friend Marcia. Tonight, however, a tall girl in slacks with short brown hair had taken that stool. The new girl stared wide-eyed at the dials and switches, her rural underbite lending her a perpetual air of vexed bewilderment.

Excuse me, whispered Vera. Where's Marcia?

Who? said the girl.

NO TALKING! barked Dr. Riley. The new girl gave a flustered look and snapped her gaze to the control panel.

Vera joined a gaggle of shift workers descending the hill to the cafeteria. Everyone travelled in groups; the compound was barely lit at night. Vera couldn't imagine why this should be. Along the coast they had blackouts against the U-boats, but here they were far from the sea. Then again, everything about Oak Ridge was strange, especially the secrecy. Nobody talked about work. Ever. Every minute someone reminded you to keep your mouth shut, and every conversation was monitored by a hovering Military Policeman.

Vera fetched her dinner from the army cooks and took a seat with the other girls.

"So Rosie, how was your night with Bill?" Eleanor teased. It was well known that Rosie had come to Oak Ridge for all the available men. Bill was her third so far.

"Boring," Rosie sighed. "He takes me to the movies, then drops me back home after. Said he had 'important calculations' to do."

"Eggheads," said Betty, rolling her eyes. "Rather figure out equations than girls."

"Have any of you seen Marcia?" Vera interjected. "She wasn't at her station tonight. There was a new girl…"

There was a pause. Rosie and Eleanor glanced nervously at each other. "Her…bunk was empty this morning," said Eleanor, voice quivering. "An MP came and took all her things."

Rosie gave a look of sudden realization. "You know," she added. "I saw her at the movies last night with some guy. The MPs came in and asked her to leave."

Betty shook her head. "Probably kicked her off the base. That girl never could keep her mouth shut."

"Girls," came a sharp male voice from behind. The women jumped. Vera turned and saw an MP looming over them.

"What were you talking about?" he asked flatly.

"N…nothing Sergeant," said Rosie, flashing a nervous smile.

"Keep it that way," the MP growled, turning on his heel.

"Actually Sergeant," said Vera. "We were wondering if you knew anything about Marcia Strong. We haven't seen her all day."

The MP stopped and slowly turned, his face grave.

"I'm sorry to inform you of this, girls," he said. "But Miss Strong passed away last night."

The girls gasped in unison.

"W…what happened?" stammered Eleanor.

"It appears she drank some bad Moonshine," said the MP.

The girls fell silent in shock.

"I trust none of you will be so reckless, or speak of this or anything else to anyone. This work is vital to the War Effort; if the enemy should ever find out about it…"

He paused and lowered his voice.

"…God help us all."

Knoxville
September 23, 1949

"…thus proving nothing can exceed the speed of light."

The Professor paused from his relentless back-and-forth pacing to erase a swath of dense calculations from the chalkboard.

"Shortly after publishing his 1905 paper, Einstein revised it and introduced everyone's favourite formula."

With great flourish, the professor scrawled a simple equation: $E=MC2$

"This states that energy is equal to mass times the speed of light squared. That's it for Special Relativity. Now on to General Relativity, which Einstein developed to factor in gravity… "

"Excuse me, Professor?" said Vera, raising her hand. The professor fell silent and squinted at her.

"Miss Mason," he said gruffly.

"Sorry, Professor, but what exactly does that equation mean? Can you give a practical example?"

"A practical example?" the professor scoffed. "I'm afraid you won't find many practical applications for Special Relativity down on the farm, Miss Mason."

The class roared with laughter. Vera blushed. Her eyes dropped to her lap. She could take the laughter. She had to. It had taken everything for her to enter this class, and she would not let her education be undermined by some pompous professor in love with his own voice. She would learn the material, regardless of the ridicule she endured.

"Well Miss Mason, let me give you a practical example," the professor said wryly as the laughter tapered off. "Can I assume you read newspapers?"

Vera nodded quickly. "Yes, Professor."

"So you know about the Atom Bomb?"

"Yes, a little bit…"

"Well," said the professor. "The first atomic bomb we dropped on Japan—on Hiroshima—had the explosive energy of eighteen thousand tons of TNT. Do you know how much Uranium that bomb used?" The professor stared directly at Vera.

"Well, n…no…" she stammered.

The professor lifted an empty artillery shell he used as a paperweight on his desk.

"Thirty-four pounds. Einstein's equation tells us that mass is just a concentrated form of energy. The amount of energy in any object is equal to its mass times the speed of light squared. Now, Miss Mason, can you tell me how many people died in Hiroshima?"

Vera shook her head.

"130,000 people. Like that," said the professor, snapping his fingers. "Vaporized where they stood. Or killed by flying debris. Or burned in the firestorm. Or died of radiation poisoning."

The professor paused for effect. The room had fallen deathly silent.

"Now," he continued. "The speed of light is a big number: one hundred and eighty six thousand miles per second. This means that a small amount of mass contains a vast amount of energy. Interestingly, not all of the thirty-four pounds of Uranium in the Hiroshima bomb was converted to energy. Most was vapourized and scattered in the blast. Do you know how much was converted to energy?"

Vera shook her head again.

"Does anyone else know?" the professor asked the class.

Silence. The professor again reached to his desk, this time producing a single paper clip.

"Three hundredths of a gram," he announced. "Less than this paper clip. That much Uranium killed 130,000 people."

A shiver ran down Vera's spine. Silence hung over the class.

"Well," the Professor finally said, breaking the tension. "All I can say is: be glad that God and Mr. Einstein are on our side!"

The class chuckled. The professor turned to the blackboard and began scrawling more equations.

"Not anymore", whispered a voice beside Vera. It was Charlie Cooper, the only boy in class who would speak to her. Also a farm boy from Tennessee, he'd joined the Air Force during the war and gotten into college on the G.I. Bill. He was a swell guy, down-to-earth and quick with a joke. But today his face was ashen, his voice grave.

"What is it?" Vera asked.

Charlie held up that day's paper. The headline filled the page.

RUSS. HAVE A-BOMB

Oak Ridge
June 21, 1945

The murmur of voices and patter of shoes grew steadily louder, drowning out the faint clicking of switches that permeated the hall. Vera leaned back as three men entered the hall: a portly man in a tan military uniform, a tall thin man with a gaunt face, and a younger man clutching a camera. The big man had stars on his cap—a General.

"Here's the control room for Beta 2, General," said the young man. "Staffed 24 hours in 8-hour shifts. We keep her humming day and night."

"Julius!" called Dr. Riley, striding down the hall. "What are you doing here? Desert too hot for you?"

"If it were, I wouldn't be coming here," said the thin man, wiping sweat from his brow. "So these are the famous girls Ed here keeps talking about?"

Dr. Riley frowned. "My hillbilly high-schoolers?" he said sarcastically. "Yeah, that's them."

The thin man leafed through a sheaf of papers. "Well, Frank," he said with a chuckle. "It seems that these 'hillbillies' are out-producing your own boys. Back in December, they produced 5.643 ounces. This past month alone, the girls produced…"

"2.215 pounds," said the young man.

"They're like soldiers," said the General proudly, beaming at the roomful of girls. "They do what they"re told and do it well. You engineers can't resist figuring out why a dial is off; the girls just fix it."

"Mr. Westcott, why don't you take a photograph of these lovely ladies?" said the thin man. The young man nodded enthusiastically. He climbed onto a nearby stool and aimed his camera down the hall.

"Smile, ladies," he said. The flashbulb popped brightly.

"Thank you, Mr. Westcott," said the General. "Dr. Riley, carry on."

Oak Ridge
July 4, 2004

A charred pocket watch, hands frozen at 8:15. Glass Sake bottles melted into tortured shapes. A woman's back, the checkered pattern of her kimono burned into her skin. Vera slowly shook her head, staring incredulously at grotesque images.

"So you can see the tremendous heat of the fireball," said the tour guide, flipping to a photograph of a broad concrete slab, marred by a large oily-black stain.

"Take this, for example," he continued. "These are the steps of the Sumotimo Bank, 250 metres from the hypocentre. That stain you see is what remains of a man, sitting on the steps when the blast hit. The heat vaporized him, leaving only this shadow."

The guide held up the photograph for a moment before tucking it back under his arm.

"Right, let's move on," he said brightly.

Bent forward in a permanent stoop, Vera slowly shuffled along with the tour group as the guide lead them around the hill. Everything was just as Vera remembered it: the high fences and guard houses, the chapel and boarding house on the hill, even the cafeteria. It was 1945 again; she could almost see the bustling crowd of engineers and soldiers milling along the grassy, sunlit paths. As the tour group rounded the corner, Vera did a double take. There, nestled between two hills, was her old building.

"This is the Beta 2 facility," said the tour guide, unlocking the door. "This contained the Calutrons, a third enrichment method used during the war to produce weapons-grade Uranium here at Oak Ridge."

More memories flooded back. The same green linoleum lined the floor, scuffed and faded with age. Tattered propaganda posters still clung to the walls. As the guide led the group down the windowless corridor, Vera was once again that nervous high school graduate, struggling to keep up as Major Winters strode impatiently ahead.

"The Calutron," continued the guide. "Named after the University of California, was really a big mass spectrometer. It vaporized raw Uranium and accelerated the ionized gas past a strong magnetic field. Because it has a lower atomic weight and therefore less momentum than U-238, U-235 was more strongly deflected and could be collected in a special compartment."

The guide paused before a massive steel door. Vera's door. The coloured bulbs above the lintel were gone, leaving empty sockets. Vera trembled in nervous anticipation.

"The Calutrons are gone, but the control panels are still here."

The guide swung the heavy door open and Vera hesitantly shuffled through. She gasped as she had sixty years ago. There they were: the old grey monoliths, standing silent vigil in rank and file down the long corridor. The hum of electricity and quiet clicking of switches was long gone. The casings were streaked with rust, the gauges yellow and dormant. But they were still standing, those panels she had come to know, love and hate for those eight months in 1945.

"The Calutrons had to be constantly adjusted and optimized," the guide continued once everyone had filed in. "At first, technicians manned the panels, but due to manpower shortages, they began hiring women—high school graduates, mostly—to run…"

As the guide spoke, he pointed to a large black-and-white photograph taped to a nearby panel. Vera's jaw dropped. There, frozen in time, was the hall as it was in 1945. Dr. Riley patrolled the hall in the background. All the girls were there, perched on their little wooden stools. In the foreground, Gladys Owens, with her slacks and timid overbite, stared hauntingly out of the photograph.

And two panels down, leaning casually back in her chair, was Vera.

Vera, in a trance, rushed forward and madly tapped her finger on the photograph.

"God in Heaven," she exclaimed. "That's me!"

"What?" said the guide, cocking his head. "That's you?"

"Oh yes!" said Vera. "Panel 857. And that's Gladys at 855."

"Well, I'll be damned!" said the guide brightly. "I had no idea you were a Calutron Girl!"

Vera frowned and slowly turned to face the guide. "I'm sorry," she said. "But what did you say this machine was for again? They never told us…"

"Oh, the Calutron separated Uranium 235 from Uranium 238…" the guide began.

Vera's old, frail body began to tremble. Tears rolled from her drooping eyes, running in rivulets down the creases of her face.

"Was…was any of that Uranium used?" she quietly sobbed.

The guide hesitated. "Well yes," he finally said. "All of it, in fact. In Little Boy…"

He paused and glanced at Vera, his face apologetic.

"…the bomb they dropped on Hiroshima."

Nashville

October 16, 1962

The glass dropped from Vera's hands as the siren blared, smashing into a hundred pieces on the tiled floor. Vera barely noticed: all she could hear was that awful, droning moan. Her heart raced. In a daze, she scrambled madly through the house. Julian wasn't in the living room, or in the lobby.

"Charlie, where's Julian!?" she cried. She heard the sliding door in the kitchen slam shut. Charlie emerged into the living room, Julian clutched in his arms.

"He was in the yard," said Charlie hastily. "Let's go." Vera nodded quickly and pulled open the basement door. They rushed down the narrow steps and ducked into the shelter, a small cube of cinder blocks in the corner of the foundation.

Charlie set Julian down on the army cot and locked the door as Vera began lighting the shelter's lanterns and candles. Even through the concrete walls, they could still hear the siren wailing up on the surface.

"Is this another drill?" she said, her voice shrill.

"I sure as hell hope so," said Charlie. "But with those Red missiles so damn close…"

"Mommy, are they going to drop the Atom Bomb?" asked Julian, fidgeting on the cot.

"No, dear," Vera assured him. "It's just a drill. Like at school, remember? We'll go back up in a few minutes."

"Mommy, who makes the atom bombs?"

"Grown-ups, dear," said Vera.

"Do you make them?" asked Julian.

"No, dear. Mommy would never do a thing like that."

··· ··· ···

With purity, holiness and beneficence, I will pass my life and practice my art. Except for the prudent correction of an imminent danger, I will neither treat any patient nor carry out any research on any human being without the valid informed consent of the subject or the appropriate legal protector thereof, understanding that research must have as its purpose the furtherance of the health of that individual. Into whatever patient setting I enter, I will go for the benefit of the sick and will abstain from every voluntary act of mischief or corruption and further from the seduction of any patient.

—The Hippocratic Oath

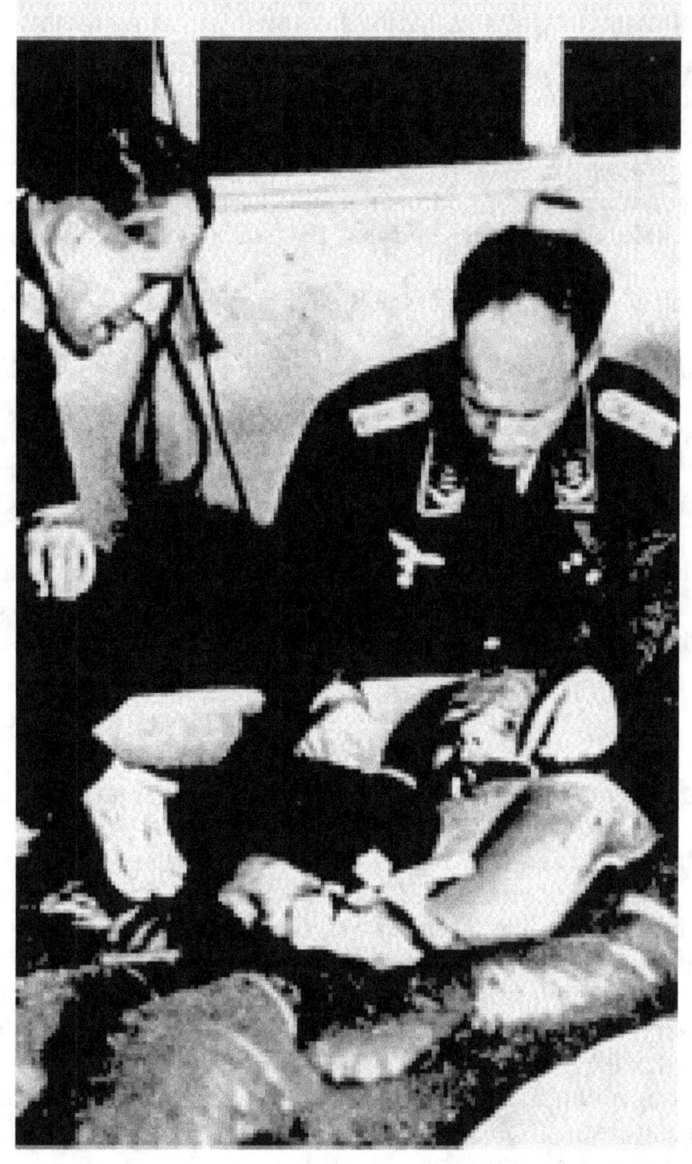

Dr. Sigmund Rascher performing hypothermia experiments, Dachau concentration camp, 1942
jmb.rsmjournals.com/content/18/1/44/F3.expansion.html

Hypothermia

HE MIGHT HAVE BEEN a piece of driftwood, or a large dead fish. The young boy's skin, blanched to a pallid, ghostly white, blended seamlessly into the kapok life vest keeping him afloat. Only the faint yellow tinge of his blond hair distinguished him from the other flotsam in the cold, dark waters.

Werner throttled back the boat's engines and carefully eased the vessel alongside the small pale shape. Approaching as close as he dared, he cut the power and scrambled from the pilot house.

"Magda, over here!" he called, leaning over the gunwales. His wife's footsteps clattered across the wooden deck as he unclasped the long boat-hook.

"No," said Magda, restraining his arm. "You might hurt him." She pulled an emergency oar from its mount and handed it to Werner.

"I've got it," said Werner, placing his hand on Magda's bulging abdomen. Magda brushed the hand away and brandished her oar. In unison they dug deeply into the frigid black water, desperately inching the craft towards the body.

"That's close enough," said Werner. "Hold me."

Magda wrapped her arms around Werner's waist as he leaned over the rail, reaching down to the body bobbing gently below. The boy, no older than five, seemed barely human, a lifeless porcelain doll. His lips and ears, a deep unearthly blue, were like inkblots on bleached vellum. His frozen arms jutted rigidly from his sides.

Suddenly, Werner hesitated, his outstretched hands trembling mere inches from the neat laces on the boy's life vest. The boy's head was arced back, as though frozen in the midst of a great yawn. The lifeless eyes in their dark, sunken orbits seemed to stare straight through Werner, up into the cold grey skies. Gazing towards heaven.

… … …

The blocks of ice made a sickly latrine sound as they fell into the test tank, the shallow, metal-lined bath in the centre of the wooden hut. Dr. Bromm knelt beside the tank and inserted his thermometer, watching as the temperature plummeted. In the far corner, Drs. Kalk and Bruhl, the Air Ministry photographers, adjusted their motion picture camera on its bulky tripod. Beside them, Frau Rascher screwed a flashbulb onto her colour camera. Seated at the table by the door, the technician busied himself with the monitoring equipment. After resetting the pens on the kymograph drum, he plunged the recording thermometer into a glass of salted ice water, watching the gauge arc towards minus eighteen degrees Celsius. Setting the thermometer aside, he opened his notebook and cleanly divided the page into crisp, uniform columns. He soon heard voices approaching from the camp outside.

"… I actually brought up that very issue with the Reichsfuhrer before I started the anoxia studies," said a bold, dominating voice. "I said: if these poor wretches survive, is that not grounds for reprieve?"

"What did he say?" said another, feebler voice.

"That these worthless creatures require no amnesty. Who am I to disagree?"

The rickety door of the hut squeaked open and Dr. Rascher strode confidently into the chamber. A man of curious contrast, Rascher would have looked the part of an ordinary, middle-aged country doctor, his dark hairline receding far back on his smooth melon of a head. But his sharp, steely gaze and black Sturmbannfuhrer's uniform transformed him into an eagle, soaring dominantly over his territory.

His conversational partner, Dr. Neff, shuffled along with downcast eyes, hands planted in his pockets. His head seemed roughly hewn from a block of wood, his mouth and eyes crude slits locked in a stony, stoic gaze. This hardened convict's face betrayed him as a former prisoner of this camp, his amnesty hinging upon his usefulness to Rascher.

The technician rose from his chair and snapped to attention.

"Sturmbannfuhrer."

"At ease," said Dr. Rascher, waving dismissively. He gazed down at the apparatus laid upon the table: recording thermometer, stethoscope, electro-cardiogram, and blood-collection instruments.

"Is everything ready?" he asked, clasping his gloved hands behind his back.

"Yes, all instruments are calibrated," the technician reported.

Dr. Bromm, kneeling by the tank, rose to his feet. "Three point one degrees," he said. "Perfect."

The photographers also nodded their readiness. Frau Rascher smiled warmly at her husband, who nodded curtly back.

"Good," said Dr. Rascher. "Bring him in."

••• ••• •••

Werner stumbled down the steep, narrow steps into the cabin, the boy's frozen, lifeless body cradled in his arms. As he unfolded the galley table and set the boy down, Magda lit the kerosene lamps.

"Is he alive?" she asked, her voice trembling.

Werner placed his fingers on the boy's neck, cold and stiff as meat from the icebox. He closed his eyes and focused, waiting for the slightest tremor, the faintest hint of a pulse.

Nothing.

"Here," said Magda, holding a small mirror close to the boy's lips and nose. Nothing. Not even the faintest wisp of vapour.

Then, somewhere deep in the stiff, frozen flesh, Werner felt it: a subtle, barely-palpable rhythm.

A pulse.

"He's alive," he announced. "Barely."

"What do we do?" asked Magda.

Werner paused, gazing at the lifeless form sprawled on the table. The neat linen trousers, the deck shoes and life vest. The bulky woollen sweater, now matted and saturated with water. The sandy blond hair that clung like wet seaweed to the boy's cherubic face.

Everything was white.

"I don't know," he said quickly, turning on his heel. "I don't know anything about these things. We need to get to shore; get him to a hospital…" He scrambled up the staircase towards the pilot-house.

"Werner!" cried Magda. "We can't just leave him like this! At least… get him out of his wet clothes…"

Werner halted in the stairwell. He hung his head and sighed.

"Yes…yes, you're right," he said, descending the staircase. Returning to the table, he untied the laces on the boy's life vest. When the last waterlogged garment was stripped off, Magda arrived with an old bundle of blankets and sweaters. Werner dried the boy's cold alabaster body and cocooned him in a thick layer of wool.

"There," he said, lowering the mummified boy onto the cabin bed. "That should stop him from losing more heat." With that, he turned to scurry up the stairs once more.

"Wait," said Magda. Werner paused again.

"I'm going to lie with him," she continued. "In the bed."

"What?" said Werner flatly.

"Warm him up," Magda explained, sitting next to the boy. "Body heat; it might buy us some time…"

Werner's face went blank, his eyes glazing over. His arms slowly fell to his sides.

••• ••• •••

The guard jabbed his rifle butt. The two women scrambled into the bed, their bulging eyes wide with fear. They were hardly recognizable as women, their sallow skin stretched thin over angular, protruding skeletons. Their breasts had long disappeared, absorbed into their empty, emaciated bodies. Whatever hair which had not been shaved hung as a sparse, tattered curtain over their skull-like faces. They were barely human, wretched beings. The male subject lay frozen and lifeless between them, his skin paler than the stained linens beneath him.

"Lie with him," said Dr. Rascher in Polish. The trembling women remained frozen, gaping at him.

"Lie with him!" Rascher shouted.

The guard cocked his rifle.

••• ••• •••

"Werner? Werner!" called Magda, snapping her fingers before his face.

Werner twitched violently, returning to reality.

"What? What did…"

"Werner, what is wrong with you?!" Magda cried. "He's dying. We have to do something!"

Silence. Only the creaking of the boat's timbers could be heard as it swayed gently on the placid waters. Magda placed her hands on her stomach.

"What if he was ours?" she said quietly.

Werner swallowed hard. "No," he said at last. "It won't work."

"What?" said Magda.

"Lying with him," said Werner, descending the steps for the last time. "It won't work. It's too slow."

Werner's eyes jumped frantically about the cabin, searching. Spying the medical kit, he pulled it down onto the table with a clatter.

"No, no, no," he muttered as he rummaged madly through the gauze, bandages, iodine bottles and smelling-salt ampoules. At last he found it: a small thermometer.

"Too slow?" said Magda, confused. "Why? How?"

"No time," said Werner, handing her the thermometer. "Boil some water. Sterilize this."

Magda hesitated, staring at Werner in shocked bewilderment. At last, however, she silently nodded and took the thermometer. Behind him, Werner heard the pop and hiss of the galley stove lighting. After a seeming eternity, the water finally came to a boil. Magda sterilized the thermometer in the water and handed it to Werner, who flipped the boy over and inserted the slender glass tube into his rectum. They then waited in strained, excruciating silence.

"Twenty-six degrees! Shit…" Werner cursed as the reading stabilized.

"What…what does that mean?" said Magda.

"We need to warm him. FAST."

"Warm him up fast? How?"

"I don't know," said Werner. "We need a bath or something."

"We don't have that," said Magda. "We…we could head back, take him to shore…"

"No: no time. He will die by then."

"But you said…"

"I know what I said, goddamn it!" roared Werner.

"Then what, Werner? Where do we put him? The bilge?"

"Maybe…"

"We can't throw him in the bilge!"

"Then what, Werner? What do we do?"

"I don't know, damn it!" Werner screamed. He frantically paced the cabin, rummaging through its cluttered contents: kerosene lamps, a bailing bucket, an ice chest, rope, mooring fenders…

"There's nothing here!" Werner cursed, kicking a pile of oilskins.

Magda's eyes dropped to the floor, then back up to Werner.

"I have an idea," she said.

… … …

The rhythmic cadence of guards' boots heralded the subject's arrival. The prisoner, a towering Russian, shuffled into the room, eyes downcast. His striped uniform hung limply from his once-hulking frame, rags on an old, spindly scarecrow.

Dr. Rascher donned his spectacles and inspected the prisoner.

"Good. A little on the thin side, but he will do."

"Strip," said Dr. Neff in Russian, his thin mouth barely moving.

The prisoner's long, bony fingers crawled like pale spiders over his chest, quickly unbuttoning the baggy shirt. As he stripped, he gazed sternly ahead, as though staring at something beyond the wall. The technician noticed his eyes. Behind their sunken, darkened sockets, they burned as though some great furnace roared in the man's head. Perhaps that was the secret of these Slavs, the technician mused; how these Bolshevik brutes could thrive on the bleak, empty steppes.

The subject soon stood naked in the middle of the hut. Drs. Neff and Bromm wasted no time, working with military efficiency. The recording thermometer was inserted rectally, and the stethoscope and electrocardiogram leads affixed to his chest. The Doctors then clothed the subject as a Luftwaffe pilot: a blue wool tunic and trousers, fur-lined leather boots, a yellow rubber life-preserver and black leather flight gloves. He hardly looked the part of the dashing ace; his shaved, emaciated head was disproportionately small atop his bulky flight gear.

"Reference temperature: 36.9 degrees," the technician announced. "Heart readings are good." The kymograph pen began tracing its narrow red line on the spinning paper drum.

"Good," said Dr. Neff, signaling to the guards. They escorted the subject to the edge of the tank, the thermometer wire trailing from his trousers like a long rat's tail.

"Get in," said Dr. Neff. Without hesitation, the prisoner scrambled into the frigid water, jostling the ice blocks that still remained.

The camera motor began to whir.

"Experiment started: one thirty-two PM," said Dr. Neff.

The technician noted the time in his notebook, then glanced to the temperature gauge: 36.7 degrees.

… … …

"There," said Magda quickly, fastening the last knot. Skirting around the hammock of oilskins that now hung from the cabin ceiling, Werner lifted the frozen boy from the galley table. Magda poured a bailing-bucket of seawater into the waterproof cradle, followed by a kettle of boiling water. She plunged her hand into the warm mixture and nodded. As Magda departed to refill the kettle, Werner laid the boy in the shallow pool. It was a crude measure to be sure, but it was the best chance the child had. Werner began sloshing water over his body, rubbing the skin to hasten the thaw. The warm fluid chilled quickly; the boy was one great block of ice.

"We need more boiling water," he said as Magda returned.

"In a few minutes," she said, placing a new kettle-full on the stove. She knelt by Werner's side, helping him rub the boy's body.

Werner shook his head. "We have to go faster. The back of his neck was in the water; he lost too much heat too quickly."

Magda inclined her head, her expression quizzical.

"What?" said Werner gruffly.

"Nothing," said Magda. "I just hope the stove lasts."

They bathed the boy for hours, replacing the warm water as quickly as the kettle would boil. Slowly colour returned to his pallid skin, banishing the sickly blue from his lips and ears. His pulse and breaths grew stronger. Then, at long last, the impossible: the boy's eyelids fluttered and he gave a faint, feeble cough. Werner lifted the boy back onto the table, dried him off, and took his temperature.

"36.5 degrees," he announced.

Magda breathed a sigh of relief. "Thank God," she said, nodding quickly. "We saved him."

"No," said Werner grimly. "Not yet."

Magda looked confused. "What…what do you mean?"

"Rewarming shock," Werner sighed.

"What?"

"Rewarming shock," Werner repeated. "It happens sometimes. The circulatory system just… collapses. I don't know why. It might happen or it might not."

Magda knelt down and rummaged through a storage locker, producing a small bottle of schnapps.

"If we can get him to drink, then maybe…"

"No!" snapped Werner. "It doesn't work."

"But everyone knows…"

"Trust me. It doesn't. It will only make things worse."

Magda was silent for several moments, staring at the bottle.

"How do you know this?" she said at last.

"What?"

Magda stared at him with red, tear-stained eyes. "How do you know?" she repeated slowly."Where did you learn all this?"

"Well, in medical school…"

"They teach these things to psychiatrists?"

"Well I…"

Werner fell silent. A thousand beautiful summers flashed before his eyes. Endless warm days by the Baltic. White beaches and warm breezes. Magda, his sparkling edelweiss, lying in the sun. Making love on a boat beneath a canopy of stars. Their children, building sand castles near the surf for all the summers to come.

"I…I worked at a ski lodge once," he stammered. "Berchesgarten, in the Alps. The patrols would always bring in… skiers, hikers…men who got lost in the snow."

"Really? When was this?" asked Magda.

"Just before the War."

Magda folded her arms, her face creasing with contempt.

"You said you worked in France before the War," she said quietly.

Werner's heart dropped to his stomach. He stood paralysed, gaping like a landed fish under Magda's darkening glare.

Then, something flashed by the porthole on the opposite wall.

"Upstairs, NOW!" said Werner.

… … …

The EKG needle jerked madly over the kymograph, forcing the technician to switch it off. The subject was shivering violently. The technician could hear his pulsing, sucking breath and chattering teeth. But otherwise he remained silent, staring stoically forward.

"He's a quiet one," said Dr. Rascher drawing a blood sample. "He should give us good data."

Indeed, thought the technician. Many of the previous subjects had screamed and thrashed as their hands and feet froze solid. Not this one: he just sat there, perfectly still as his consciousness slipped away.

"34.2 degrees," the technician announced.

"Good," Dr. Rascher nodded. He glanced at the technician.

"What is your name, Gefreiter?" he said after a few moments.

"Mohr, sir," the technician answered. "Werner Mohr."

"Where are you from?"

"Wismar, sir."

Dr. Rascher grinned. "I know it well," he said wistfully. "Lovely beaches; many wonderful holidays."

Across the room, Frau Rascher beamed.

"Tell me, Gefreiter" said Dr. Rascher placing his fingers on the subject's neck. "Do you have a sweetheart waiting somewhere?"

"No sir," said Werner.

"A shame," said Dr. Rascher. "Thirty-two beats a minute."

Werner marked the reading on his data table, then set down his pen. It had been two hours. The subject now appeared paralysed, his jaw locked in a mask of barely-veiled agony. Werner could hardly imagine the plight of all those brave Luftwaffe pilots, surviving the fury of air combat only to freeze to death, alone in the open sea. It was an ignoble end for a brave warrior; perhaps this Slav and his kin would turn the tide against this silent, frigid enemy. New protective clothing could be invented, or new methods for rewarming the frozen. The possibilities were endless.

Every half hour Dr. Rascher drew another blood sample, a task which grew ever more difficult as the subject's body drew blood towards his core, clutching for warmth ebbing inexorably away. Rascher removed the subject's glove: his hand was pure white, like porcelain.

The subject ceased to shiver. He bobbed gently in the tank, only the faint expansion of his chest and an occasional blink betraying life. His arms were bent, his hands protruding from the water in some grand questioning gesture. As his heartbeat ebbed away, his head curled back and his eyes stared directly upwards, straight through the roof of the hut. Gazing towards heaven.

… … …

A fishing boat materialized from the thick fog. Werner could not believe his fortune; a moment later and he would have missed them in the haze. As the boat approached, Werner spied two people—a man and a woman—standing on the prow.

"Ahoy!" the man called. "Have you seen a boy? Six years old, blonde hair!"

"Yes!" cried Magda, rushing to the rail. "He's here! He's safe!"

"Oh thank heavens!" the woman cried, clasping her hands over her mouth.

"Catch hold," called Werner, tossing over a line. Within minutes the family was scrambling over the rail.

Werner, lead them down the stairs. The mother fell to her knees, grasping her son's tiny hand as she whispered a prayer.

"He still needs to be taken to a hospital," said Werner, nervously pacing the room. He found his pipe on a nearby shelf and lit it. With trembling hands, he brought the stem to his lips and took a deep draught. "It's a miracle we found him when we did. Any longer and…"

The father nodded slowly, his eyes welling with tears. "Sir, we…we can't thank you enough…"

Magda's footsteps beat like a funeral drum as she descended the stairs. Arms folded, she glared at Werner.

"Nonsense," said Werner, reining in his wavering voice.

"I'm a doctor…it's what I do."

... ...

Patriotism is when love of your own people comes first; nationalism, when hate for people other than your own comes first.

—Charles de Gaulle

French Foreign Legionnaires charging at Bir Hakeim, Libya, 1942
en.wikipedia.org/wiki/File: Free_French_Foreign_Legionnairs.jpg

Képi Blanc

Bir Hakeim, Libya
May 25, 1942

WHAT A PLACE to fight a war. A sea of sun-baked stone stretched unbroken from horizon to horizon: a vast expanse marred only by an endless speckled carpet of dark stones, unperturbed by even the slightest hillock. The cruciform shadow of the Junkers transport aircraft sailed smoothly over the ground below. It was a wonder anyone could fight here, in this wasteland forsaken of cover, shade and water. Yet fight they did, and fought well. The horizon bore witness to this remarkable feat: a tiny white cloud, easily dismissed as a sandstorm, rose from the desert floor in the distance. That humble wisp betrayed a storm of a different kind: the rolling steel of the Afrika Korps, thundering across the empty, scorched wastes.

Always on the move, thought Feldwebel Gerhardt Hentschel, smiling. The flat expanse, he mused, was a vast chessboard, on which the Feldmarshall played his deft, deadly gambits. He turned to face his brigade. They were in good spirits: sharp, keen and well-rested from a week's leave in Italy. Six months ago they had nearly pushed the British out to sea at Tobruk; now they had returned to finish the job.

Glancing out the window, Gerhardt saw a new cloud rising into the azure sky: an ominous black column of burning gasoline. The tiny desert airfield ahead was littered with the charred corpses of aircraft, like dark cigarette burns in the sand. Ground crews scurried about like ants below.

The Junkers swooped down onto the airstrip with a spine-shattering impact, stirring a stifling cloud of dust that filtered in through every seam in the fuselage. As the aircraft ground to a halt, the brigade leapt to its feet and filed out into the searing Libyan sun.

They jogged towards the Panzer column parked outside the airfield, through a frenzy of scrambling crewmen and air thick with dust, aviation fuel and the roaring din of propellers. Gerhardt pulled down his sand goggles.

"What's all this?" he called to a Luftwaffe man running past.

"Damned SAS!" said the crewman before rushing off.

Gerhardt glanced back at his men. "They won't be laughing tomorrow!" he boasted.

Reaching the column, the crews separated and mounted their vehicles. Gerhardt affectionately patted the faded white palm tree stencilled on his Panzer III before hoisting himself through the turret hatch. Standing in the commander's cupola, he donned his radio headset as his crew took their positions. At last, the signal to advance crackled over his headphones.

"Forward," said Gerhardt, rapping his knuckles on the turret armour. The bestial growl of engines rumbled through the column, followed by the metallic squealing of tracks as the vehicles lurched forward. On the radio Gerhardt heard a faint, tinny voice humming Panzerlied. Within minutes, the entire column had joined in, belting out a rousing chorus as the spearhead thrust its way toward Egypt:

> Ob's stürmt oder schneit, ob die sonne uns lacht
> Der tag gluhend heiss, oder eiskalt die nacht
> Versaubt sind die gesichter, doch froh ist under sinn
> Ja unser sinn
> Es braust unser panzer im Sturmwind dahin

… … …

Algiers, Algeria
July 14, 1958

The eerie wail of the meuzzins floated down from the minarets, filtering through the narrow, winding alleys like a ground fog. At once the city came under its hypnotic spell. In the streets and markets, the faithful knelt as one. A low drone of incantations answered the call from above as a shining white sea of humanity rose and fell in great swells on the pavement. In the main square, however, their professions went unheard, drowned out by the rattle of drums, the sharp cadence of marching boots and the jubilant cheers of the pieds noirs gathered on the sidelines in linen suits and flower-print dresses. Through the square flowed another white river, not of diaphanous burnouses or niqabs but of shining starched képis as the 1st Foreign Parachute Regiment marched triumphantly into Algiers.

"Regiment, halte!" barked Lieutenant Colonel Jeanpierre, the Regimental Commander. As the marching boots clicked to a sudden halt, the crowd's fanfare quickly tapered away.

"Band! Képi Blanc!" called the Colonel. In the ranks, Corporal Gerhardt Hentschel swelled with pride. It was the same tune which had rung out from the Panzers all those years ago. The lyrics had changed, but he and his fellow Legionnaires still sang with the same heady vigour:

Puisqu'il nous faut vivre et lutter dans la souffrance
Le jour est venu où nous imposerons au front
La force de nos âmes, la force de nos cœurs et de nos bras
Foulant la boue sombre, vont les képis blancs

"Legionnaires," the Colonel addressed them as the song ended. "Company commanders report to HQ at 16:00 hours for briefing. Until then you are dismissed. Remember, you are always on duty; you will aid the army and police in maintaining order whenever necessary. Honneur et Fidelité! "

"Honneur et Fidelité!" came the deafening affirmation.

"Legionnaires, dismissed!"

Some hours later, sporting their green combat fatigues, Gerhardt and his comrades set off towards the Casbah. As the Legionnaires ventured deeper into the city, they entered a different world. The crooked streets grew ever narrower and darker, plunging them into a strange perpetual twilight. This was the antithesis of the open desert: a battlefield of nothing but blind corners, traps and hidden exits. There was barely room to swing a rifle. This claustrophobia was made worse still by the chaotic crush of people choking the narrow alleys. Black-robed women scurryed about with groceries; youths on scooters and bicycles; old men smoking hookahs in the shadows. Merchants locked in passionate bartering matches amid the technicolour palettes of the spice shops. This chaos, Gerhardt knew, was the ultimate redoubt: invisible and ephemeral, yet as impenetrable as any concrete bunker. A gunman could swiftly vanish into this crowd, leaving the Legionnaires to shoot at mirages. Gerhardt grew uneasy; it was Berlin all over again. His eyes flitted from alley to doorway to window as he compiled his battle plan, preparing for any possible ambush.

"You alright, Boche?" asked Corporal la Tour. Gerhardt scowled; he hated that nickname. Ever since his enlistment it was always L'Allemand or Boche.

"I'm fine," he grunted, lighting a cigarette. "Just an ugly place for a firefight."

"Never stop working, do you?" laughed la Tour. "Relax! One day here, then it's off to the mountains."

"That's good," Gerhardt grumbled.

"Bonjour, mademoiselles! Ca va?" chirped Corporals Jimenez and Johannsen as a knot of young women shuffled past. They roared with laughter as the women jabbered angrily in Arabic.

"You'd think they weren't happy to see us," said Johannsen, grinning. Indeed, in stark contrast to the parade ground, here the Legionnaires met nothing but hostile glares from the native Algerians.

"Well, they'd better get used to us," said Gerhardt, donning his sunglasses. "Once we mop up the FLN they'll have to get used to the idea of being part of France."

Jimenez and Johannsen eyed Gerhardt strangely.

"Christ, Boche," chuckled Jimenez, shaking his head. "You've been listening to too many of de Gaulle's speeches."

"I make it a point to remember why we're here," said Gerhardt matter-of-factly. "Maybe you should too."

The four men walked in strained silence for several moments before Johannsen broke the tension.

"Well, on the bright side," he said. "You couldn't ask for better weather."

"Better than Indochina," said la Tour, glancing up at the sky peeking between the whitewashed walls.

"How would you know?" asked Jimenez. "You were in reserve like the rest of us."

"My brother, Francois," la Tour explained. "Said he didn't see a day without rain."

"What unit?" asked Johannsen.

La Tour shook his head. "The First…bought it at Dien Bien Phu."

"My condolences," said Jimenez.

"His own damn fault," said la Tour. "Joined because he wanted 'adventure'. He certainly got it…"

"Adventure," said Gerhardt sarcastically, flicking his cigarette butt to the cobblestones.

"Hey Boche, why'd you join?" asked Jimenez. "Couldn't get an Argentine visa?"

"Long story," mumbled Gerhardt. "Let's just say I'd rather be fighting with us than against us."

The Legionnaires soon entered a small open square, dominated by the ancient red-brick walls of the Casbah. Two blue-uniformed gendarmes manned the barbed-wire barricade blocking the gate, directing the human traffic into the ancient citadel as paratroopers in green helmets and berets stood guard nearby.

"Come have a drink," said la Tour, beckoning Gerhardt to a nearby cafe table.

"We're on duty," Gerhardt objected.

"Yes," said la Tour, dropping heavily into a chair. "But I doubt having lunch violates our mandate."

"I guess it's true what they say about the Germans," joked Jimenez. "You can have fun, but only when someone tells you when and where!"

The Legionnaires shared a hearty chuckle.

"Another time," said Gerhardt flatly. "I think the checkpoint officers need all the help they can get."

"Suit yourself," said la Tour, flagging down a waiter.

Gerhardt shook his head as he marched away. These men were all fine soldiers, but they rarely took their duties as seriously as they should; in this volatile environment, they could not afford to let their guard down. Reaching the checkpoint, Gerhardt nodded to the gendarme on duty.

"Afternoon, Corporal," the gendarme mumbled distractedly as he inspected an identity booklet.

"Good afternoon," said Gerhardt. "Anything to report?"

The gendarme shook his head and flagged a citizen through.

"Very quiet this morning. It's been…"

He was interrupted by a chorus of whistles and catcalls from the paratroopers as a gorgeous young woman with dark almond eyes and raven hair floated past. Glaring angrily, she clutched her handbag and hustled quickly through the checkpoint, disappearing into the dark labyrinth of the Casbah.

Gerhardt did a double take. "Why didn't you check her!?" he asked, incredulous.

"Oh, she comes through here all the time," said the gendarme, shrugging.

"What about her handbag?" Gerhardt pressed. "She could be carrying a pistol…"

The gendarme shook his head. "The women don't carry the guns. They hide the terrorists, cook, gather intelligence, fetch supplies, carry messages…by the way, do you have a smoke?"

"Yes," said Gerhardt absently, reaching to his pocket. He frowned as he stared through the barricade.

"Thanks," said the gendarme, flicking open his lighter. "Believe me, Corporal, you learn very quickly how the FLN…"

Suddenly, a thunderous detonation rocked the square. The hammer blow of the blast wave knocking Gerhardt to the ground. A great plume of flying debris erupted from the cafe, filling the square with a great roiling cloud of dust. In a daze, Gerhardt clumsily scrambled to his feet, his hands fumbling over the cobblestones for his rifle. Squinting down the barrel, he swept the weapon in spasmodic jerks around the square. His ears rang, drowning out the screams of the fleeing crowd. Through the haze he saw a bloody, uniformed figure stagger out from the gaping maw of the shattered cafe. The man lurched forward a few agonizing steps, then collapsed in a heap amid the rubble.

··· ··· ···

Bir Hakeim
May 25, 1942

Generalleutnant Crassmann, 15th Panzer Division Commander, paced restlessly before the large map pinned to the wall of his tent.

"The Abwehr reports the British taking up positions here, here and here," he said, tapping the paper with his baton. "At dawn, the 150th Infantry and Italian 10th and 20th Corps will attack Gazala. We, with the 21st Panzer, Trieste and Ariete Divisions, will drive south to engage the Free French position here, at Bir Hakeim."

Crassmann swept his baton in an 'X' motion over the dot marking the tiny Oasis.

"Those of you who fought in France—as I did—will know, we should make short work of them," he said, grinning wryly. Laughter rumbled through the Panzer commanders gathered in the tent.

"Past Bir Hakeim," Crassman continued, "we will turn North, cutting off the British eastern flank. The 150th is then free to capture Tobruk, drive to Egypt…and take the prize—the Suez Canal. Any questions?"

The commanders unanimously shook their heads.

"Zero-hour is 7:30," Crassman concluded. "Dismissed."

Gerhardt shivered as he stepped out into the evening air; it was still strange to him how cold the desert could be at night. Hands deep in his pockets, he tramped back between the dormant, moonlit hulks of tanks and halftracks. He soon found his comrades Helmut and Walter playing cards by the glow of an oil-drum fire. He sat down, and Helmut poured him some coffee from a thermos.

"Thanks," said Gerhardt, savouring a warm draught. It was then that he noticed the two strange figures huddled in the corner. They looked like Bedouin with their thick beards with Arab headdresses, but their khaki tunics betrayed them as British soldiers. Military policemen with brass gorgets on their necks stood guard.

"Who are they?" asked Gerhardt.

"SAS raiders from the airfield," said Walter. "Jeep ran out of gas, so they stayed back to raise hell."

"I heard that they ran out of ammunition and explosives," added Helmut. "So they tore out the instrument panel from one of the Messerschmitts with their bare hands!"

"Crazy bastards." Gerhardt shook his head. "We'll have an easier time with the Frenchies tomorrow."

"Maybe," said Helmut warily. "But I've heard things about the Legion to make your hair stand on end."

"Bah!" scoffed Gerhardt. "With three Panzer divisions, we'll give them a beau geste of their own!"

Walter smirked. "To a beau geste!" he toasted, raising his tin cup.

They were interrupted by approaching footsteps as a Colonel arrived with a squad of soldiers. He wore the same tropical uniform as the other officers, but his collar runes and Totenkopf cap badge marked him as an SS man.

"That's them?" the Colonel asked his entourage, pointing to the SAS prisoners. The soldiers nodded.

"You," the Colonel called to the MPs. "Stand them up." The prisoners slowly rose to their feet, glaring contemptuously as the MPs prodded them with their rifles.

"What's going on?" whispered Gerhardt, glancing curiously at his comrades.

"I don't know," said Helmut warily. "But let's not rattle the Butcher Bird's cage…"

But Gerhardt had already risen. "Oberst," he said. "What's going on?"

"Nothing that concerns you, Feldwebel," said the Colonel distractedly. Drawing his pistol, he gestured to the MPs to bring the prisoners forward.

"What's being done with the prisoners?" Gerhardt pressed. "Does General Crassmann know of this?"

The Colonel gave an irritated sigh. "If you must know, Feldwebel, the Fuhrer has issued direct orders to execute any commandos captured. Now return to your business." He gestured again to the MPs.

On the ground, Walter and Helmut frantically beckoned Gerhardt to sit back down.

"You can't do that, Oberst," Gerhardt blurted. Helmut and Walter winced and shook their heads: don't.

"What was that!?" snapped the Colonel, stopping in his tracks.

Gerhardt swallowed hard. "Oberst," he said slowly. "These prisoners are under Army jurisdiction, not SS. Standing orders from the Feldmarshall are that the Geneva Convention is to be followed."

"Forgive him, Oberst," said Walter, springing to his feet. "The…anticipation of battle is getting to him."

The Colonel smirked, producing a notebook and pen. "What is your name, Feldwebel?"

"Gerhardt Hentschel," said Gerhardt, pulling away from Walter's grasp. "15th Panzer Division."

"Feldwebel Hentschel," said the Colonel. "If you don't wish to be brought up for insubordination, I'd advise you to drop this matter. I'm sure the Feldmarshall needs all his best men for tomorrow."

"Drop it…" hissed Walter.

Gerhardt ignored him. "I'm sorry," he said forcefully. "But it is my duty to inform my superior officers of this." He turned on his heel and began marching away.

"Sergeant, arrest that man," ordered the Colonel. An MP marched towards Gerhardt, weapon drawn.

"Leave him," said a sharp, authoritative voice. "The prisoners as well, Oberst."

Wheeling around, Gerhardt was astonished to see Feldmarshall Rommel—the Desert Fox himself—standing at the edge of the clearing. In the shadows, he cut an imposing figure, his long great-coat like the cape of some Wagnerian demon. But as he stepped closer to the fire, the flickering light revealed a more modest visage, a face that reminded all of their father or a cherished uncle. Beneath a receding wisp of hair, his normally sharp, calculating eyes betrayed a deep, distant weariness.

"Feldmarshall," the Colonel saluted. "With all due respect, this is an SS matter. We have our orders."

"I've read them," said Rommel bluntly. "And while this Corps remains under my command no such orders will be carried out. I have already made this quite clear."

"Indeed," said the Colonel. "And many are growing impatient at your refusal to follow direct orders. I will be including this incident in my report."

"Please do," said Rommel.

Frowning, the Colonel waved off the MPs and saluted again. "By the way," he added, pointing to Gerhardt. "Keep an eye on him: he's an idealist, that one."

Turning on his heel, the Colonel strode off between the dark silhouettes of the vehicles.

The men stood in silence. Rommel, hands clasped behind him, gazed contemplatively at the moon.

"Get some sleep," he said quietly to the men. "You will all need it for tomorrow."

Gerhardt nodded: thank you. Rommel inclined his head, then wandered back into the night.

"Shit, that was close," Walter cursed as he sat back by the fire. "Do us a favour, will you Gerhardt? Screw around with the SS on your own damn time! I don't want to die of dysentery in the Tunis camp."

Gerhardt said nothing. Striding past, he snatched up Helmut's thermos and handed it to the prisoners. They took it with a silent nod of thanks.

"What the hell?" exclaimed Helmut. "What's gotten into…"

He stopped mid-sentence, eyes flying to his wristwatch.

"It's starting!" he exclaimed. "Quick, go!"

Walter sprang to his feet and disappeared with the others into a nearby communications tent. The grating static and unearthly wails of the radio blared over the loudspeaker, soon giving way to a deep, soothing voice.

"…this is Radio Belgrade, 7:00 P.M. 25th May, 1942. And now, for our brave troops, wherever they may be fighting, the incomparable voice of Miss Lale Andersen."

Sitting down, Gerhardt leaned back and closed his eyes as the silky, lovesick strains of Lili Marlene floated out over the camp. A low, droning chorus built as the men hummed along with the tender ballad, this tantalizing piece of the Fatherland reaching out to them through the aether. And in the corner, the prisoners slowly swayed as they sang, in their own language.

Vor der Kaserne,
Vor dem großen Tor,
Stand eine Laterne,
Und steht sie noch davor,
So woll'n wir uns da wieder seh'n,
Bei der Laterne wollen wir steh'n,
Wie einst, Lili Marleen.

… … …

Algerian-Tunisian Border
September 1, 1958

Gerhardt ducked behind the Jeep's dashboard as a mortar round exploded nearby. Sand and blasted rock clattered off his helmet. These sparse barrages, fired blindly from the Tunisian border, were little more than a nuisance. The true threat lay in the village below, a motley array of whitewashed shacks clustered around a dusty goat-path that snaked past a well and a date-palm orchard. Squinting down the barrel of his machine gun, Gerhardt watched the green figures creep silently down towards the village, dodging between the low scrub and rocky outcrops. Nothing stirred in the tiny hamlet; the Legionnaires had achieved complete surprise. Gerhardt grinned. There would be no café bombings here, no hit-and-run shootings in a crowded Souk. This was a proper battlefield; the skirmish ahead would be one of coordination and manoeuvre, just as they had trained.

At the signal, the Legionnaires charged in. At once the symphony of combat erupted: the tinny rattle of submachine guns, the sharp crack of rifles, the dull reports of grenades. This violent cacophony blazed barely a minute before abruptly tapering away. The roaring echo rolled away down the valley, giving way once more to the whistling wind and eerie chorus of buzzing cicadas.

Suddenly, something stirred in the village. Gerhardt spotted a quartet of men slithering out a rear window. As they scurried towards the orchard, Gerhardt reached for the radio handset.

"Rebels fleeing town!" he signalled. "Heading for the orchard!"

"Open fire, goddamn it!" came the angry command. Gerhardt hastily drew a bead and pulled the trigger, the weapon juddering painfully against his shoulder. The tracers arced low, biting at the fleeing men's heels. Gerhardt swept the stream of lead forward, sending three rebels crashing to the rocky ground. The fourth dodged into the orchard and disappeared, leaving the bullets to splinter the swaying trees. Gerhardt released the trigger.

"Three down, one in the orchard," he radioed. Two Legionnaires gave chase, but soon emerged from the orchard empty-handed.

Within minutes the squad had regrouped by the vehicles. Major Beaudrillard, the squad commander, stormed angrily towards the jeep, sunglasses glinting menacingly in the noon sun.

"Who fired on the runners?" he growled.

Gerhardt snapped to attention. "I did, Major."

"Why the hell did you call it in!?" Beaudrillard snapped. "You had a clear shot; the bastard's probably on his way to warn the whole goddamn valley!"

"I wanted to avoid friendly fire," Gerhardt explained matter-of-factly. "Standard procedure."

"Standard procedure?" hissed Beaudrillard. "Brilliant, Sergeant. You've probably cost us the damn…"

He was interrupted by a low moaning sound as two Legionnaires crested the hill, dragging a wounded Rebel between them. He was a boy, no older than 17, with dark, bushy eyebrows and wild, fiery eyes. His shattered ankle bled profusely, leaving a dark red trail in the pale dust.

Lieutenant Daumier, the medic, rushed through the crowd as the Legionnaires propped the prisoner up against the jeep. He worked quickly, tourniqueting the leg and staunching the bleeding with forceps.

"Leave him," said Beaudrillard flatly, stepping up to the prisoner. Daumier made to object, then hesitantly nodded and backed away. The prisoner glared up at Beaudrillard, eyes burning with malice.

"Where are the rest of your friends hiding?" said Beaudrillard, lighting a cigarette.

Silence.

"I won't ask again," the Major repeated slowly, removing his sunglasses. "Where are they?"

The prisoner continued to glare defiantly.

Beaudrillard sighed. "You!" he called, pointing to Gerhardt. "Interrogate him."

"Me, sir?"

"Yes you, Sergeant!" Beaudrillard growled. "Make it quick!"

Gerhardt dropped to his knees. Pulling the canteen from his belt, he wetted his hand and passed it over the prisoner's sweaty brow.

"Feels good, doesn't it?" he said softly. "Now, tell us where your friends are and we can get that leg looked at. Get some morphine for the pain. Sound good?"

"Sergeant, what in the hell are you doing!?" roared the Major, storming over.

"Interrogating the prisoner, sir…"

The Major snatched the canteen from Gerhardt's hands. "I said interrogate him, not play nursemaid!"

In one swift movement, Beaudrillard brought his heel crashing down on the prisoner's shredded ankle. The boy's shrill, terrifying scream echoed through the valley. His face a grotesque, contorted mask of pain, he writhed and convulsed in the dust.

"Five minutes!" said Beaudrillard, spitting on the ground. "Didn't the Gestapo teach you anything?"

"Sir, I was never in the…" said Gerhardt.

"Shut up!" the Major interrupted. Gerhardt fell silent. The other Legionnaires began crowding around, staring as the prisoner panted and gasped on the ground.

"What the hell are you waiting for?" hissed Beaudrillard. "Get on with it."

"No, sir," said Gerhardt.

"What did you say?"

Gerhardt stood and snapped to attention. "Sir, I will not torture this prisoner."

Beaudrillard shook with barely-contained rage. "Legionnaire," he said. "That was a direct order."

"I'll do it," said Sergeant la Tour, stepping forward. Beaudrillard thrust out a blocking hand.

"I didn't ask you," he said, still staring at Gerhardt.

"Sir…" started Gerhardt. His eyes flitted to the other Legionnaires, who stared back disapprovingly.

"Sergeant, I won't ask again. Interrogate that prisoner…"

"Major," interrupted Lieutenant Daumier. Beaudrillard snapped his head to face him. "With all due respect, sir: he's right. We don't tort—"

A spurt of blood erupted from Daumier's throat as a bullet slammed home. Eyes bulging, he drew a raspy, gurgling gasp before collapsing to the ground, blood bubbling from his lips and down his face.

"Sniper!" The Legionnaires dropped to the ground, scrambling for cover behind the vehicles. Stepping over the prisoner, Gerhardt grabbed his rifle from the jeep and trained it on the hills overlooking the village. The Legionnaires waited in strained silence, the sun beating down mercilessly on them through the dusty, stagnant air. Daumier lay writhing and gurgling out in the open, but nobody dared approach him. Mercifully, another bullet slammed into his chest, ending his suffering.

"Where did it come from?" called Beaudrillard as the echoing rifle crack caught up with the bullet. The Legionnaires squinted through their gunsights, frantically scanning the hills.

"I think I…" someone announced before a bullet tore through his forehead. His skull burst open like an overripe melon, unleashing a crimson geyser of blood.

Up in the hills, Gerhardt spotted the muzzle flash.

"There!" he shouted. "Under the overhang, 11 o'clock!" The Legionnaires unleashed a furious volley, saturating the craggy hills with lead. Up on the crest of the ridge, a tiny shape slumped out from behind a boulder and plummeted down the valley wall, twisting and flailing limply like a rag doll.

The Legionnaires ceased firing.

As the roar of the barrage faded to silence, Gerhardt heard a strange sound: a rhythmic, wheezing rasp. Glancing about, he soon found the source.

The prisoner was laughing.

Sprawled on the rocky ground, his chest heaved in great spasms as he flashed the broadest of smiles. A cruel grin, full of condescension and disdain. He stared at Gerhardt with amusement, slowly shaking his head as if he—and he alone— were privy to an unspoken farce, the greatest joke on earth.

Without thought, without hesitation, Gerhardt raised his rifle butt and smashed it into the boy's face.

… … …

Bir Hakeim
May 26, 1942

Gerhardt raised his field glasses and surveyed the battlefield. There was little to see: Bir Hakeim was little more than a dusty crossroads, barely warranting a spot on the map. Only the crumbling shells of the old fort walls and the small green smudge of the oasis proper distinguished the place from the tractless wastes all around. But the wind-blasted rock and shifting sands, Gerhardt knew, hid a hive of carefully-hidden trenches, foxholes and minefields. Through his glasses, Gerhardt caught brief glimpses of white Képi caps peeking above the trench rims, gleaming in the morning sunlight. Legionnaires.

Gerhardt dropped down through the Panzer's cupola, closing the hatch behind him. Pressing one eye to the periscope, he viewed the fort as he would during the upcoming fight. Pulling away, his eyes fell upon the old photograph he kept pinned to the gun stabilizer. Through the cracks and creases in the faded sepia print, his father—an old cavalryman— gazed boldly from atop his horse, a formidable figure in his sharp Prussian uniform and Kaiser moustache. If only the old man could see me now, leading the charge, thought Gerhardt..

A chain of thunderous roars signalled the start of the artillery barrage. Tall geysers of sand and smoke erupted all over the fort. The small shapes of men scurried madly between the blasts, like termites fleeing a smashed nest. The dust soon smeared into a uniform haze, cloaking the fort like a fog.

"8th Brigade, advance!" the order crackled over the radio. Gerhardt grabbed his throat microphone and relayed the command, shouting above the din of the barrage. The engine roared as the vehicle lurched towards the lines. Through the periscope, Gerhardt saw the Italian tanks charging up ahead, their commanders strangely comical in their flamboyant black-tasselled caps. The infantry advanced alongside, crouching low by the vehicles' flanks. Gerhardt surveyed the lines; according to the engineers, the French had left a narrow passage through the minefields ringing the fort. The barrage should have widened the gap, but they could not count on this. Speed was key; only by exploiting this initial confusion could they cross no-man's-land before the French brought their heavy guns to bear.

Suddenly, the German guns were answered by a new, sharper staccato as the French artillery opened fire. A nearby blast rocked the vehicle, nearly knocking Gerhardt from his seat. As a further wave of shells exploded all about in quick succession, Gerhardt swung open the hatch and poked his head from the cupola. To his horror, he saw a tight barrage of mortar shells fall into the thick of the charging infantry, tearing entire companies apart in an instant. The sharp rat-tat-tat of machine guns rang out from the trenches, the pale tracers mercilessly raking the column. Up ahead, an Italian tank burst into flames, swerving crazily before grinding to a halt.

"Take aim at the gun positions!" yelled Gerhardt as he slipped back into the turret, pressing his eye to the periscope. "26 degrees left. Elevation: 3 degrees. Fire!"

Gerhardt clapped his hands over his ears as the main gun fired, reverberating deafeningly through the hollow steel chamber. The shell grazed the gun pit, exploding harmlessly behind it.

"Reload!" he ordered. "Re-acquire and…"

"Third and fourth brigades falling back!" came a frantic cry over the radio. Springing once more through the cupola, Gerhardt saw the infantry abandoning them in droves, fleeing back to their lines.

"15th, Ariete, Trieste, pull back! You are without infantry support!" The order was met only with animated jabbering as the Italians continued to brazenly charge the French lines.

"Commander, we have to fall back!" exclaimed Manfred, the driver.

Gerhardt winced as bullets clanged loudly off his turret. He glanced to the photograph by the periscope.

"No!" he replied. "Keep advancing! If we can take out the guns, the infantry can adv-"

Directly ahead, another Italian tank exploded. The Panzer veered sharply away in a wide arc.

"Manfred, turn back!" Gerhardt shouted frantically. "Get back into the corridor! We're in…"

A violent concussion hammered into the bottom of the vehicle, sending the 23-ton tank rearing upwards. Gerhardt slammed into the turret ceiling. A paroxysm of pain flashed through his body as he crashed into the ammunition rack below. As he painfully clambered back into the turret, he felt warm blood flowing over his face. The vehicle appeared intact; they had hit a mine.

"Bail out!" Gerhardt yelled, reaching for the escape hatch. They were dead men here; better to brave the small arms fire than be obliterated by artillery in this steel coffin. Glancing through the periscope once more before abandoning ship, Gerhardt saw the flash of an anti-tank gun.

Another detonation ripped through the hull, sending a searing wave of fire through the vehicle. The turret instantly filled with black, acrid smoke. Gerhardt hacked violently; his lungs burned in the fetid cocktail. He flailed blindly for his submachine gun, his hands clanging over the levers and cranks crowding the cramped turret. It wasn't there. But as he reached again for the hatch handle, his hand brushed over a sliver of paper. The photograph. He quickly snatched it as he threw his full weight on the hatch, diving into the clear air beyond. As rifle bullets ricocheted around him, he dropped to to the desert floor. Pressing himself flat to the ground, he crawled frantically away as his vehicle erupted into a roman candle of exploding fuel and ammunition.

… … …

Algerian-Tunisian Border
September 1, 1958

The prisoner's confession led the Legionnaires to a small limestone cave behind the orchard. Two sentries guarded the entrance, but a brief volley sent them scurrying back into the tunnel.

"Now the eternal question," said Beaudrillard, stepping up to the portal. "How do we get the rats out of the hole?" He was answered by a chorus of metallic clicks as a group of Legionnaires stepped forward, pulling the pins from their grenades. They grinned with great relish as they tossed the deadly spheres—the very symbol of the Legion—into the dark maw. The dull reports resonated hollowly through the chamber beyond. A thin cloud of pale dust lazily rolled out into the sunlight. Striding back to his jeep, Beaudrillard grabbed a megaphone and marched back up to the cave.

"This is Major Beaudrillard of the 1st Foreign Parachute Division!" he barked. "Come out with your hands on your head or we will eliminate you to the last man!"

There was no response.

"Again, sir?" asked a Legionnaire, brandishing a grenade.

The Major shook his head. "There's a bend after the entrance," he said, glancing into the cave. "They're behind it. We'll have to blow the entrance." He nodded to a squad of sappers waiting nearby, unmistakable with their thick beards. Their chief, Lieutenant Castor, shook his head.

"We don't have any more explosives," he said. "We'll have to go back to El-Oued to get them."

"No time for that," said Beaudrillard. Hands on his hips, he stared at the ground, deep in thought.

"Bottle them in," he said after a few moments. "Get what you need from town."

As the other Legionnaires stood guard, the sappers fetched bricks and mortar from the village and began sealing up the cave. They whistled and joked as they worked, as though they were building some garden wall. Sitting on a nearby boulder, Gerhardt shook his head and turned away. Raising his canteen, he took a long draught. His hands trembled; water sloshed out and was quickly lapped up by the thirsty earth. A great weight pressed on his chest, as though a poisonous snake had curled around his heart. He did not understand; in twenty years of military service, he had seen countless men die in every terrible manner imaginable. He had seen their faces, full of agony and terror. But they were all swiftly borne away on the stream of memory, for such was the nature of war. Gerhardt had never felt a twinge of anxiety, nor lost a moment of sleep. But where all those faces had faded to oblivion, one lingered: the Algerian boy, eyes burning with the hatred of an entire nation…

"Boche!" snapped la Tour, sitting nearby. Gerhardt twitched and turned back to face the cave.

"Pay attention! What the hell's the matter with you today?"

Gerhardt shook his head. "Nothing."

La Tour spat into the dust. "Well, whatever it is, you'd better pull your head out of your ass. Your messing about got Daumier and Godard killed today."

"That's fucking bullshit and you know it!" growled Gerhardt, throwing his canteen to the ground. It knocked over his satchel, spilling the contents over the ground.

"That sniper was probably there for hours," Gerhardt grunted as he knelt and gathered his possessions. "He would have gotten someone either way. That prisoner knew nothing about it."

"But maybe if you hadn't…hmm, what have we here?" said la Tour, reaching for a book that had fallen from Gerhardt's satchel.

"Kreig Ohne Hass," read la Tour. "By Erwin Rommel. I'm afraid my German's a bit rusty…"

"Give it back," said Gerhardt.

Ignoring him, la Tour plucked out a tattered photograph from between the pages and held it up to the light. At this, Gerhardt snatched the book back and stuffed it back in his satchel. He turned away and sat in silence, watching the sappers raising the brick barrier ever higher.

"It means War Without Hate," he finally sighed after a few moments.

La Tour snickered. "You really came to the wrong place for that, Boche."

There was another long pause. "That was my father," said Gerhardt. "First Hussar Cavalry. Only fought once: at Mons, right at the start of the War. His first charge…and his entire squad: gone. Mowed down by machine guns." He swept his hand in a wide arc and made a rat-a-tat machine gun sound.

"Sorry to hear it," said la Tour, his voice flat, disinterested.

"Oh, the lucky old bastard survived," said Gerhardt. "They got him in the leg, but the horse fell on him. Cut off the bleeding. But he never did get over it. Sad way for a cavalry man to go: gunned down from halfway across the field by some conscript cowering in his trench. Not even brave enough to get up and face him man-to-man…"

Gerhardt trailed off, his gaze sweeping over the Legionnaires gathered around the cave. They smoked, chatted and laughed nonchalantly as the cave dwellers were slowly sealed in their premature tomb, their Cask of Amontillado.

"Twenty nations in the Legion," he muttered. "Yet those ones are rats…."

"I don't know about you," said la Tour. "I can tolerate rabbits, squirrels and moles in the garden…"

He turned sharply towards Gerhardt, revealing the jagged white scars and wrinkled grey burns that pockmarked his face—the handiwork of the café bomb.

"…but I can't stand the rats."

La Tour was interrupted as the sappers pulled away from the cave. Lieutenant Castor slathered the last brick with lime and pressed it home, completing the wall. Once the mortar had set, Major Beaudrillard stepped up and struck the barrier several times with his rifle butt.

"They're not going anywhere," he said, grinning wryly. "Let's move out."

With that, the Legionnaires mounted their vehicles and pushed on along the dusty mountain trail. There was a loud throbbing as a helicopter soared overhead, hugging the valley walls like some giant, sinister dragonfly. In the distance, a roiling napalm fireball erupted with a deep roar as another village was wiped from the map. But as the dark column of smoke rose into the clear sky, the bright strains of Le Boudin, the Legion marching song, echoed clearly through the valley:

Tiens, voila du boudin, voila du boudin,
voila du boudin
Pour les Alsaciens, les Suisses et les Lorrains
Pour les Belges y en a plus,
pour les Belges y en a plus
Ce sont des tireurs au cul

… … …

Bir Hakeim
May 26, 1942

Burning fuel and shards of metal rained down all around. Gerhardt gritted his teeth as he manically crawled from the shattered tank, his elbows scraped raw on the sharp rocks. Bullets whistled mere inches above his head. But by some miracle, he came upon a small shallow ditch, barely large enough for one man. Crawling in, he peered over the lip and scanned his surroundings. The French guns roared a stone's throw from his dugout; the German lines, by contrast, seemed a thousand miles away, past a hellish sea of burning vehicles and shell craters. Gerhardt reached to his belt; his tiny Walther pistol was all but useless here. Braving the long dash across no-man's-land was suicide, he concluded; better to wait until the French lines were overrun.

With a loud rumble, a squad of German halftracks lunged forward, towing a battery of 88 mm guns. Braving a hail of bullets, the crews leaped from their vehicles and assembled their weapons with clockwork discipline. Gerhardt grinned: the French defences could not match this powerful weapon.

But then a frightening barbarian cry roared out from the French trenches.

"Legionnaires! Marche ou Crève!"

A swarm of Legionnaires spilled from their foxholes and charged the German artillery, along with a handful of small-tracked Bren Carriers. Gerhardt pressed himself to the ground, feigning death as the boots trampled all around him. The Legionnaires covered the open ground with astonishing speed, swiftly taking up positions behind the burned-out tanks. The 88's opened fire, obliterating a lightly-armoured Bren Carrier. The Legionnaires pressed on, picking off the gun crews with rifle fire. The guns roared again. An 88mm shell sailed across no-man's-land, landing squarely in a nearby

French gun emplacement. The concussion pounded Gerhardt's ears; the emplacement disappeared in a fountain of blasted sand and limbs. But when the dust settled, one man remained standing, his arm torn off above the elbow. Bloodied and burned, he staggered up to the intact gun and loaded a shell with the stump of his arm. He then fell to his knees and tugged the firing cord before tottering forward, dead. The gun reared back. The shell whistled across the battlefield and destroyed the 88. The crews abandoned their guns, the Legionnaires raking them with fire as they scrambled back to the German lines.

What is this madness? Gerhardt was incredulous: the Panzers were in full retreat, racing back into the desert. The Legionnaires cheered triumphantly; inside the fort, a whistle called them back.

Gerhardt cursed. He was alone, stranded behind enemy lines. He could not tell when the next attack would come, and in any case he doubted he would last that long. The sun had not yet reached its zenith, and he had neither shade nor water. Drawing his pistol , he glanced over to the gun pit, where a squad of soldiers was busy clearing away the dead. If he could keep the gun crews distracted, he thought, perhaps the Panzers could finally break through. It was a suicidal plan, but there were few other options. Under siege with limited supplies, the French were hardly in a position to take prisoners. Whatever the outcome, this would earn him the Knight's Cross.

Gerhardt glanced at the photograph in his hand before tucking it into his pocket.

This is for you, Father, he thought, springing from the ditch. The soldiers in the emplacement froze, gaping incredulously. Bridging the gap in seconds, Gerhardt vaulted the trench wall and opened fire, the pistol snapping pathetically amid the din of battle. A round blasted cleanly through a Legionnaire's skull, the blood spatter staining his white képi. Gerhardt swung frantically about, firing blindly into the confused mob. Then something smashed into his skull with a sharp crack, sending him crashing to the ground. In a daze, he found himself staring down the barrel of a rifle as a gaggle of scruffy, bearded soldiers stared down at him in disbelief. An officer mumbled some orders and two Legionnaires dragged him away to the rear of the fort. Gerhardt stared up at one of the soldiers, who trained his submachine gun on him.

"Faites…le," he said in his rudimentary French. "Do it."

But the Legionnaire did not shoot. Silently, he lowered his weapon and reached into his pocket, producing a single cigarette in a tattered wrapper. This he handed to Gerhardt, along with his canteen.

"Merci," said Gerhardt.

The Legionnaire smiled.

… … …

Maison Blanche Airfield, Algeria
April 26, 1961

A bead of sweat rolled down Major Gerhardt Hentschel's face. The glass-walled terminal was a veritable greenhouse; the ancient fans beating lazily overhead did little to abate the stifling heat. Gerhardt wiped his brow and turned to face the platoon of Legionnaires occupying the departures hall. He sighed and shook his head. The past year had taken its toll: only a handful of men remained from the original contingent that had landed in '58. They had even lost the formidable Major Beaudrillard two months ago when his helicopter was shot down over Algiers. But the Legionnaires' will was strong as ever, even if that of the politicians in Paris was not. But all that would change, and very soon. The radio crackled and wailed as Lieutenant Phare, the signals officer, struggled to reach the Regimental Commander.

"Colonel Saint-Marc, this is Maison Blanche Airfield. Are you receiving? Over."

"What's taking so long?" Gerhardt growled, restlessly pacing the hall. "We should have gotten an answer by now…"

"Sorry, sir," said Phare, shaking his head. "Their receiver must be switched off."

"Keep trying," said Gerhardt. Phare nodded.

"You've failed," called a heavily-accented voice.

"Who said that!?" snapped Gerhardt, wheeling around. He glared at the airport staff, held hostage and seated on the departures benches with their hands on their heads.

"I did," said an airport guard.

"Sergeant," said Gerhardt to the Legionnaire guarding the hostage. "If that man utters one more word, you are authorized to bind and gag him."

"What?" scoffed the guard. "Did you really think you could retake the country by yourselves? Your whole army couldn't do it in ten years!"

"Shut up," said Gerhardt bluntly.

"Face it," the guard continued defiantly. "You are finished! Algeria belongs to its people! Your own people agree with us. Go back to your country and leave us ours!"

Gerhardt drew his pistol and swung it hard, the butt connecting sharply with the guard's skull. The man collapsed in a heap onto the faded, scuffed linoleum

"Not on my watch," hissed Gerhardt, looming overhead. "Not after all we have sacrificed for this place. Not while our blood stains the sand."

"My people have bled too," gasped the guard, blood trickling from the gash on his brow. "And we…have won…"

Gerhardt raised his pistol again.

"Major…" interrupted a voice behind Gerhardt. He turned to see a Legionnaire sitting nearby, a transistor radio pressed to his ear. Ashen-faced, he slowly shook his head in disbelief.

"Sir, check…check the Citizen's Band…" he stammered.

Gerhardt strode up to a ticket counter and switched on a radio. The crisp diction of a news broadcast echoed clearly through the terminal:

"…announced this morning that the attempted coup in Algeria has collapsed. Following President de Gaulle's speech five days ago, in which he sought the support of the French people and army, it has been reported that all branches of the armed forces have confirmed their allegiance to the President. Only the 1st Foreign Parachute Regiment, which seized control of Algiers six days ago, has remained defiant. Earlier this morning, the ringleaders of the coup—Generals Zeller, Jouhaud, Salan and Challe—surrendered in Algiers. President de Gaulle assured the people of France that the remaining putschists would soon be brought to justice. In other news, at 6 O'clock this morning…"

"It's over," said the guard on the floor, grinning smugly through his mask of blood.

"Sir!" called a sentry by the window. A column of green military vehicles had rolled onto the apron and disgorged a platoon of soldiers. Within seconds they took up positions around the airfield, completely surrounding the Legionnaires. An officer emerged from a truck and raised his megaphone.

"Major Hentschel! This is Lieutenant-Colonel Roland of the 1st Parachute Chasseur Division. By order of Monsieur Pierre Messmer, Minister of the Army, the First Foreign Parachute Regiment is hereby disbanded. You are surrounded; release your hostages and come out without weapons!"

Gerhardt stood by the window for a long time, staring at the thin line of green dotting the sun-bleached concrete. But he finally turned to face the terminal. He nodded to the hostages, who rose and filed out onto the tarmac. Two clerks lifted the bloodied security guard and carried him out the door.

Gerhardt faced his men. "I suppose this is it," he said. "Not how I had imagined it. But no-one can say we didn't try. No-one can say we didn't fight for France. Legio Patria Nostra!"

"Legio Patria Nostra!" the Legionnaires called back.

Throughout the terminal, the men began removing their weapons and equipment, laying them in neat piles on the floor. Gerhardt knelt and rummaged through his satchel. He saw a flash of white: tucked beside his tattered copy of Krieg Ohne Hass was his dress képi. He pulled it out and held it up to the light. He could not remember the last time he had worn it; over the past three years it had become crusted with dust, sand and dark brown spatters of dried blood. Slipping off his beret, he raised the old, stiff cap and pressed it to his crown. All around him, his fellow Legionnaires followed suit, turning the terminal into a sea of white. Gerhardt stood, leaving the book at his feet.

"Platoon, form a parade column," he barked. "File out, quick march!"

The Legionnaires quickly lined up along the terminal. Gerhardt marched to the head of the column.

"If I see anyone raise their hands, I will kill him myself."

They marched from the terminal into the hot Algerian sun, as proudly as they had arrived all those years ago. And over the lonely airfield echoed that beautiful song Madame Piaf had dedicated to them just days before. It was their song now, and it rang truer than ever.

Non, rein de rien
Non, je ne regrette rien
Ni le bien que on m'a fait
Ni le mal
Tout ça m'est bien égale

An American war correspondent standing in the rubble of Hiroshima, Japan, September 1945.
theatlantic.com/infocus/2011/10/world-war-ii-the-fall-of-imperial-japan/100175/

Obelisk at Trinity Site, New Mexico - site of the world's first nuclear detonation July 16,1945.
[Sama Jain Photo, October 2, 2010.]
flickr.com/photos /tamasrepus/5079553260/

Part II

A

Is

For

Atom

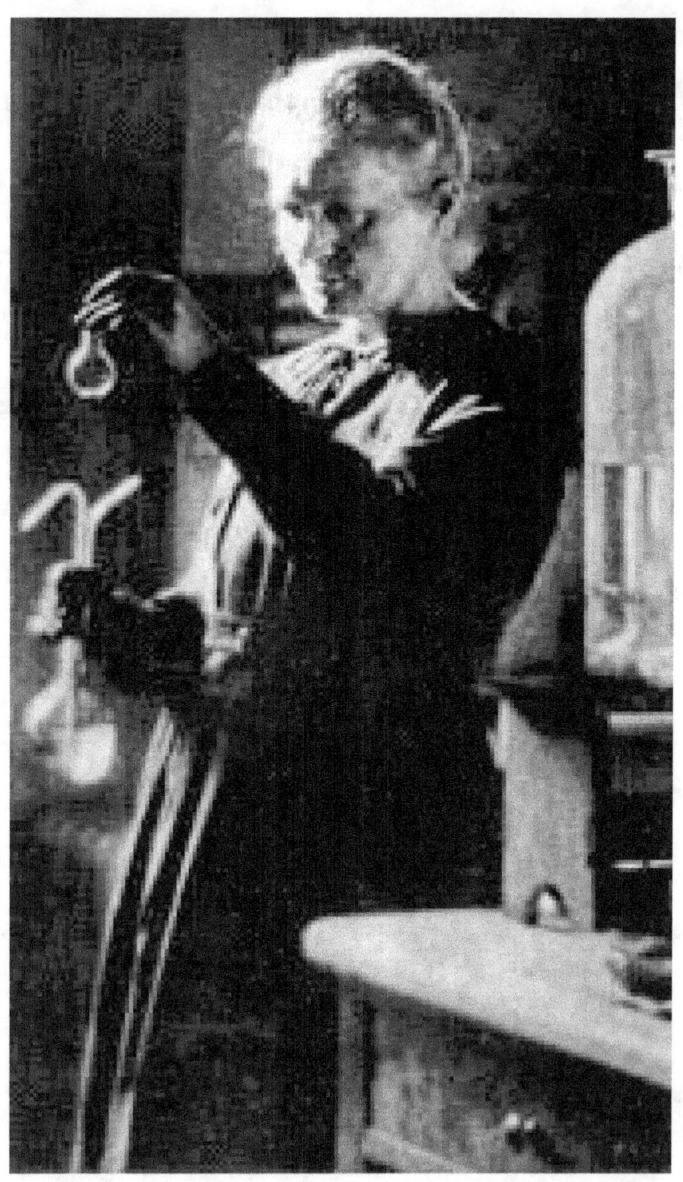

Marie Curie in her laboratory, University of Paris, 1925
clinchem.org/content/57/4/653/ F1.expansion
["International Year of Chemistry 2011: A Test of Courage: Marie Curie and the 1911 Nobel Prize" Clinical Chemistry, April 2011]

... ...

Technology is a gift of God. After the gift of life it is perhaps the greatest of God's gifts. It is the mother of civilizations, of arts and of sciences.

—Freeman Dyson

For a successful technology, reality must take precedence over public relations, for Nature cannot be fooled.

—Richard Feynman

The release of atomic energy has not created a new problem. It has merely made more urgent the necessity of solving an existing one.

—Albert Einstein

Cleanup of the Three Mile Island nuclear power plant, 1979.
en.wikipedia.org/wiki/File: TMI_cleanup-2.jpg

Foreword: Atomic Reactions

ALL GENERATIONS have their miracle technologies. In the mid-19th Century, Chemistry was King, heralding a limitless future of artificial dyes, plastics and medicines. All of humanity's ills, it seemed, could be remedied by rearranging a few chemical bonds. Soon, the mystical power of electricity seemed to promise mankind the ultimate secret —the spark of life itself. Miraculous restorative powers were ascribed to electricity; in Mary Shelley's Frankenstein, it could reanimate the dead. In the latter half of the 20th Century, we drew even closer to the ultimate secret as genetics gave us the power to manipulate life at its most fundamental level.

But honeymoons inevitably end, and the awed public soon grew disillusioned and suspicious. Dreams of chemical fertilizers, electronic luxury and custom medicines became nightmares of pollution, cancer from high-tension power lines, and genetically-engineered chimaeras. But one technology stands apart in its swift and near-total fall from grace. That technology is nuclear power.

From its discovery in the late 19th Century, radioactivity acquired an almost supernatural mystique. Radioactive rays could pass through flesh and bone without hindrance. They could generate light that never went out. Solid matter could vanish into thin air. One element could spontaneously transmute into another—the ancient quest of the Alchemists. Unsurprisingly, many ascribed miraculous powers to radioactivity. Radium was added to cosmetics to give the user a 'glowing' complexion, and millions flocked to natural radium hot springs for their supposed rejuvenative powers. The health benefits of radiation were touted well into the 1950s, with physicist Edward Teller stating "it may be…that some radiation is good for you." In the midst of this craze, many legitimate uses for radioactivity were also discovered. X-rays allowed doctors to peer into the body without risky explorative surgery, and radiation therapy saved countless from the death sentence of cancer.

But the true heyday of radioactivity awaited one of the greatest breakthroughs in physics: the splitting of the atom. In 1942, in a squash court beneath the University of Chicago, the first self-sustaining nuclear chain-reaction was initiated. Three years later, the first atomic bomb was detonated in the New Mexico desert. Atomic fission unlocked the true potential of the atom, placing vast amounts of energy at mankind's fingertips—one kilogram of Uranium replaced a thousand tons of coal. In the optimistic climate of post-war America, the Atom was the future. Nuclear power plants sprang up all over the continent, promising electricity too cheap to meter. Ford even announced plans for the Atomica, a nuclear-powered car.

But the public's honeymoon with nuclear power nearly ended before it began, as horrific images from Hiroshima and Nagasaki began filtering back home. The atom had a dark side. The bombings would also inspire an icon of the nuclear age: the B-movie atomic monster. In 1954, Toho studios of Japan released Godzilla, about a prehistoric monster mutated by nuclear testing who terrorizes Tokyo. Unlike its more cartoonish sequels, the original 1954 film handles its subject matter somberly, showing in explicit detail the human toll of atomic warfare. The dangers of nuclear weapons would be underscored in 1956, when the first American Hydrogen Bomb, Castle Bravo, was detonated over Bikini Atoll in the South Pacific. The device produced a massive cloud of radioactive fallout that poisoned many native Marshall Islanders and the crew of a Japanese fishing boat. As the cold war escalated, a dark atomic shadow loomed over civilian life.

On March 28, 1979, a stuck valve at the Three Mile Island nuclear power plant in Pennsylvania triggered the partial meltdown of the reactor. Seven years later, an explosion at the Chernobyl power plant in Ukraine unleashed a massive radioactive cloud that spread over vast tracts of Europe. In March 2011, a massive earthquake and tsunami in Japan lead to the meltdown and explosion of four reactors. In the wake of each incident came a fresh wave of anti-nuclear sentiment. The number of reactors being built each year has tapered to almost nothing. Nuclear had become a dirty word.

This is the classic story told of nuclear power: the story of how mankind, in his hubris, tampered with the forces of nature and paid the tragic price. It is the mythology behind an entire movement, whose attitude was best expressed by musician Pierre Schaeffer: It's ridiculous that time and time again we need a radioactive cloud coming out of a nuclear power-station to remind us that atomic energy is extraordinarily dangerous. Yet like all mythologies, this one is rife with falsehood and exaggeration. Indeed, the entire nuclear movement is grounded in the roots of hysteria: ignorance and fear of the unknown.

The main conceit of the anti-nuclear movement—that nuclear power is inherently dangerous—is based off a handful of extreme cases. The two greatest nuclear disasters both resulted from outdated or poorly-designed reactors being pushed far beyond their design limits. The Chernobyl reactor was a dangerously unstable Soviet design, cheaply and expediently built and subject to extreme operator error. The Fukushima plant, 30 years old and 10 years overdue for decommissioning, was built in a known earthquake and tsunami zone without adequate safeguards (the other 53 reactors in Japan survived). And while the Three Mile Island incident (also the result of errors in reactor design) resulted in millions of dollars of damage to the plant, it released negligible amounts of radioactivity into the environment. Indeed, the incident might not have become a byword for nuclear disaster had the film The China Syndrome not been released two weeks before. The film, a conspiracy thriller about a near-meltdown at a nuclear power plant, was eerily prescient of the real-life disaster and was instrumental in turning public opinion against nuclear power.

This is not to say that nuclear energy harbours no danger whatsoever. However, if the mere existence of danger were sufficient to damn any technology, we would still be living in the stone age. Statistically speaking, cars and airplanes are far more dangerous than nuclear reactors, and as technology evolves, safety improves. Every single major nuclear disaster has occurred in a reactor built before 1990; indeed, over 30% of all reactors currently operating are 30 years old or older. After every nuclear disaster, countries panic and cease to build new reactors. Unable to forfeit generating capacity, however, they continue to push their existing reactors beyond their service lives and in the process court disaster. The proper reaction to nuclear disasters, paradoxically, would be for countries to build more reactors. Nuclear technology has come a long way since the 1970s, and modern reactor designs are safer than ever. For example, the Canadian-designed CANDU is all but impossible to melt down, and can burn an extraordinary range of nuclear fuels. Such modern reactors, however, incur high up-front costs, which deter many nations who instead opt for cheaper—and more dangerous—traditional designs.

The supposed radiological dangers of nuclear power plants are also largely exaggerated. In fact, burning coal releases more airborne radionuclides than nuclear power under normal operation. Radioactivity itself might even be less dangerous than many suspect. In the 1980s, a steel company in Taiwan accidentally melted down a medical teletherapy machine containing radioactive Cobalt-60. The contaminated steel was made into rebar and used to build nearly 2,000 apartments, exposing the residents to over 100 times normal background radiation. When the error was discovered 15 years later, a study was conducted to determine the rates of cancer and birth defects among the residents. Strangely, the rates were found to be 95% below the predicted values. Further research revealed that moderate radiation doses can actually be beneficial, stimulating the cellular-repair mechanisms that help stave off cancer. Edward Teller might have been right after all.

It can thus be seen that in the field of public discourse, misinformation reigns. While the fundamentals of radioactivity and atomic fission are not difficult to grasp, many continue to view nuclear power as a mysterious, unknowable force, a mystical force to be feared. But as fossil fuels become depleted and the demand for clean energy mounts, nuclear power is poised to take centre stage once more. Solar, wind and tidal energy—the darlings of the anti-nuclear movement—are still in their infancy and cannot efficiently supply our energy needs. Nuclear is the only clean energy source of sufficient capacity available to us. It cannot be denied that nuclear technology has been misused and abused in the past, but we have the ability to remedy past mistakes and put this tremendous power to the best possible use. The time has come to embrace the atom once more.

For better or worse, the atom has dominated the history of the Twentieth Century, influencing nearly every aspect of our daily lives. With the stories collected in this volume, I attempt to capture this enormous impact and inspire the reader to become more informed on the subject of nuclear power. After all, only when informed can we make proper decisions. In these pages I have traced the tumultuous trajectory of the atom from its discovery to its possible future: promise and innocence, corruption and eventual redemption.

··· ··· ···

'In that case,' answered the Genie, 'know that presently thou wilt have to die.' 'Heaven forbid!' cried the fisherman; 'Or, at least, tell me why! Surely it might seem that I had done thee some service in releasing thee.'

—From A Thousand and One Nights

Hand and Atom advertisement, c.1950s
ultraswank.net/science/our-friend-the-atom—-part-1

The Fisherman and the Genie

ADAM RUSHED IN through the front door. He carried on straight through the house, not bothering to remove his shoes or drop his backpack.

"Hi Mom!" he announced.

"How was school?" came the listless voice from the living room.

"Fine," said Adam. It was an automatic exchange, a ritual, conveying that once again Adam had not been hit by a truck on his way to school. He could have aced a test or been beaten half to death by bullies, and his day would still have been 'fine'. Adam did not bother Mom with anything but trivial answers; she was always so tired. In the darkness of the living room he caught a glance of her inert form sprawled over the sofa, silhouetted in the flickering blue light of the TV. There she would remain for another two hours , watching her 'soaps' until Dad arrived. Only then would she scrape together whatever passed for dinner. Adam glanced at the clock: he had three hours. Feeling the weight of the backpack digging into his shoulder, he pressed on, pausing briefly as he noticed the dirt he was tracking through the house. He shrugged, doubting Mom would notice or care. Stepping out the back door, he wondered why they called those shows 'soaps'. He had sat through several episodes and never seen any soaps, only grown-ups in dimly-lit rooms holding boring conversations. Grown-ups were strange.

Adam emerged into a brown, overgrown tangle that had once been a garden. It occurred to him that he had never seen Mom or Dad do any gardening; they barely found the time or energy to even mow the front lawn. But Adam didn't care about ivy or rosebushes; his destination was the potting shed tucked in the corner of the yard. Wading through the waist-high weeds, he picked up a stick and hacked his way forward like some intrepid explorer. He had asked Mom and Dad for a machete once. They had flatly refused.

Adam braced his shoulder against the shed door and threw his full weight against the grey, rain-weathered wood. It gave way with a tortured, splintering squeal. In the musty gloom beyond, scurrying mice fled between moldy bags of grass seed. The shed was near collapse, its moss-crusted walls leaning at crazy angles. The roof had rotted through in places; shafts of sunlight pierced the dusty, mildew-tinged air, lending the cramped space the vague air of a cathedral. The effect was most appropriate, thought Adam, for this was his sanctuary, his temple to science and discovery. His laboratory. Skewed shelves by the broad wooden potting bench held a motley assortment of scratched, smoke-stained flasks, beakers, and jam jars full of chemicals. How long had it taken him to amass this inventory? Two years now. Two years of pleading with Mr. Toews, his science teacher, for every piece of damaged or outdated laboratory equipment, every expired bottle of chemicals. Months of staking out the science lab garbage can, snapping up whatever Mr. Toews would not part with willingly. Countless hours in stores, scouring cleaning products labels for the elusive reagents he required. It was taxing work, made all the more so by the need to conceal it from his parents. His first attempts at chemistry, employing kitchen utensils as makeshift labware, had resulted in burns on the kitchen counter and a month's grounding. On one rare occasion when Mom had more energy than usual, she had allowed him to experiment with baking soda and vinegar—albeit under her close watch, wearing gloves and goggles. Though he appreciated the gesture, he had been bored to tears; he craved real chemistry. Now, so long as he could smuggle his equipment through the house, he was free to experiment as he pleased. Mom and Dad never ventured into the back yard, and as far as they knew, the shed was simply a quiet place for Adam to read.

Adam's backpack slid off his shoulder, making a muffled thud as it hit the dirt floor. Adam knelt and upturned the bag, emptying its load of dark crushed stones onto a large pile in the middle of the room. He had been smuggling this material for a year now, under the pretense that it was part of his rock collection. Mom and Dad had accepted this explanation without question; a rock collection, after all, was a perfectly safe, acceptable hobby for a twelve-year-old boy. Had they known their geology, though, they would have known that the greasy black rocks with streaks of dirty yellow had no place in a respectable rock collection. But this mineral, Pitchblende, was more valuable to Adam than the most flawless diamond. This stone held a powerful secret. Locked beneath its ugly, greasy exterior was the greatest power in the universe: the mighty power of the atom. A veritable witch's brew of exotic elements—Uranium, Thorium, Polonium, Radium—lay within, awaiting only a skilled mind to release them from their tenacious chemical bonds. Adam knew he was such a mind. Ever since discovering that outcrop of Pitchblende in the woods near school, he knew it was his unwritten duty, his destiny, to extract the elements within. It would be the ultimate demonstration of his knowledge and skills, a right of passage. Purifying Radium at his age would win him the endless admiration of Mr. Toews and untold prestige elsewhere. He bore no illusions, however, as to the difficulty of his task, especially with the crude tools at his disposal. Thankfully, he would not be alone in his endeavor. As Newton had once said, he stood on the shoulders of giants

Turning from the rock pile, Adam faced the wooden shelf roughly nailed above the potting bench, which held his most prized possession: his collection of science books. He ran his finger affectionately over the cracked and faded spines, as if greeting old friends. This collection too had been a long time in the making, painstakingly compiled from library trash cans and bookstore discount bins. The books were all 50 years out of date, their covers torn and their pages yellow and dog-eared. Yet Adam would not trade them for the newest textbook hot off the press. They were his constant companions, the patient guides who had ushered him into the wondrous world of science: Birth of the Universe, Elementary Chemistry, Life on Earth, The Life and Times of Albert Einstein, Particle Zoo. But his prized possession, occupying a coveted spot on his shelf, was The Life and Work of Marie Curie, by Roberta Frolich. With reverence usually reserved for holy books, Adam gingerly slid the volume from the shelf and laid it out before him. The binding had long ago disintegrated, leaving a tattered folio of stained sheets barely clinging to a spine of peeling cellotape. The latter half of the book had been lost before Adam rescued the remainder, but this mattered little. He had long searched for a proper scientist's book, a detailed but clear guide to the advanced experiments he so desperately wished to challenge. But all the Chemistry books he could find were dry and impenetrable. The science books written for children his age were even worse, filled with nothing but vague generalities. Vital information was always omitted, seemingly with the intention of frustrating Adam's ambitions and smothering him in saccharine safety warnings. This book was different, seemingly written with Adam in mind. It was a relic of the 1950s, an apparent golden age that praised boldness and innovation, and accepted risk in science as unavoidable. Scattered among the passages detailing Madame Curie's extraordinary life, the author had included extraordinarily detailed descriptions of her laboratory techniques. Carefully turning the pages as one would an illuminated medieval manuscript, Adam laid open the greatest wonder contained within: a full chart explaining Marie Curie's process for purifying Radium. This diagram had been Adam's guiding light for the past year, like a pirate's map leading him to buried treasure. He ran his finger over pages smudged from countless consultations, following the bewildering, branching tree of boxes and lines. The process was long and convoluted: crush ore and treat with sodium carbonate, dissolve in sulphuric acid, boil with sodium hydroxide, treat with hydrochloric acid … it was easy to lose track. Missing a single step would leave him with an impure mess of random elements; it had to be right the first time.

Adam's heart fluttered as his finger glided down the page. Only one step in the process remained: fractional crystallization. Tonight, he would see the culmination of a year's patient, determined toil. Tonight, at long last, he would isolate Radium. Reaching to the corner of the shed, Adam pulled away an old burlap sack, revealing a large cider jug hidden beneath. The jug sat in a cooking pot full of water, whose temperature had been precisely regulated by an aquarium heater. Floating in the jar was a strange object, which looked for all the world like a giant furry white worm suspended in formaldehyde. Adam, however, was no mad biologist; the worm was merely a twisted piece of coat hanger, encrusted in countless white, needle-like crystals. The complex purification process had, in the end, yielded only that jar of fluid, a solution of Radium and Barium Carbonate. These two compounds were similar, differing only in the temperature at which they crystallized. By precisely controlling the temperature of the solution, Adam could ensure that only the Radium crystallized, leaving the Barium behind. Adam reached for the coat hanger, then stopped. An alarm clock perched on his bookshelf indicated that twenty minutes remained in the twelve-hour crystallization session. It was a minor difference, but Adam could ill afford to cut corners. Not this close to the end. So he withdrew his hand and waited. The decision was a painful one; he had waited all day for this, his mind wandering distractedly through all the dull, rote lectures. His mind had been singularly focused upon this one moment, anticipating it more than any Christmas morning. In response, the clocks had all conspired to slow themselves down.

To pass the time, Adam turned to the menial work that had dominated his year: crushing ore. Lacking even a mortar and pestle, he shoved several handfuls of Pitchblende into a burlap sack and proceeded to pound it with a hammer. He then transferred the resulting gravel into a saucepan and ground it to fine powder with a screwdriver handle. It was during this painstaking task that he felt closest to Marie Curie and her husband Pierre. They too had labored for years in a makeshift laboratory such as this, tirelessly processing tons upon tons of Pitchblende to extract mere milligrams of Polonium and Radium. Adam, of course, was merely following a recipe; the Curies had actually invented it. He gazed in awe at the complex flowchart: how one could devise such an intricate process from scratch was beyond him. Perhaps one day he would be capable of such feats, but in the meantime there was no shame in following a recipe; if there were, there would be no master bakers or chefs. Adam's accomplishment would be like baking a perfect soufflé. But no chef, Adam mused, had ever faced challenges as he had. Few master bakers had to grow their wheat and grind flour, or raise chickens and cows for eggs and milk. But Adam, lacking a chemical storehouse, was forced to procure vital reagents by methods varied and ingenious. Sulphuric acid from discarded car batteries, Sodium Hydroxide from laundry lye, Potassium Nitrate and Hydrochloric acid from gardening and hardware stores. Adam was reminded of the story of Hercules and the Hydra, which his teacher had once read to the class. As when one of the Hydra's heads was cut off, two more would grow in its place, so it seemed that when Adam solved one problem, many more appeared. His greatest challenge was obtaining chemicals with no commercial sources, which had to be pleaded from Mr. Toews's closely-guarded stores. It had taken much ingenuity to devise sufficiently plausible—and harmless—experiments requiring these chemicals, and much grace under pressure to convince his increasingly suspicious science teacher. Only once had he ever stolen a chemical—Iron Sulphide—but he vowed to replace this theft when his project was complete. Surely once he had isolated Radium, Mr. Toews would forgive his indiscretion; he had, after all, acted in the name of Science.

The alarm rang, signaling the end of crystallization. Adam's hand immediately leapt for the cider jug, his heart racing with excitement. This is it, he thought, slowly lifting the encrusted wire from the solution. He had done it. In his hand he now held the most beautiful object he had ever seen. Radium, Marie Curie's greatest accomplishment, was now his as well.

As Adam withdrew the wire, his arm brushed the meat thermometer immersed in the water bath. He froze: the needle had dropped three degrees. The thermometer, he realized in horror, had been stuck the entire time. His heart sank as he laid the wire down. Had he failed? Had the Barium also precipitated, contaminating his Radium? This was to have been his night of triumph, when all came to fruition. Would he have to start over, wait through another endless night and day? No, he thought. He couldn't wait. He had to have his success tonight. But how to know if he had succeeded? He had no means of determining his sample's purity, not even a Geiger counter—the vital tool of any nuclear physicist. Above all else, Adam coveted a Geiger counter. He had scoured every laboratory catalogue he could find, but found no model in his price range. As per usual he had asked Mr. Toews for one, but had suddenly found himself at the end of Toews's patience.

"What do you possibly need a Geiger Counter for?" he had asked, his eyes narrowing suspiciously.

"Radon," was Adam's response. "My basement might have a Radon leak. I thought it would be cool to check."

"Then your parents should buy a detection kit", Mr. Toews snapped. "I think I've given you more than enough equipment already, don't you think? More than I should. The principal would have a fit if he found out. No: no more, Adam. That's enough with the experiments. I will not be responsible for you killing yourself."

"I won't kill myself, promise. I'll be careful!" Adam pleaded. "I know what I'm doing."

"No you don't", said Mr. Toews dismissively. He would discuss the matter no further. Desperate, Adam had resorted to begging his parents, pledging to double his chores or forsake his birthday presents. For his trouble he received a bicycle and baseball bat, useless implements now gathering cobwebs in the corner of the shed. Adam was thus reduced to using an electroscope, a crude instrument he assembled from a flask and some tinfoil. In theory, Alpha and Beta particles streaming off a radioactive element would impart a static charge on the instrument, causing the tinfoil leaves within to spread apart. But as Adam swept the instrument over the white crystals, the leaves remained stubbornly limp. No matter what he tried, the instrument refused to work. He had now but one recourse: the phosphor test. Adam hesitated; if he used this test, he would face weeks of painstaking purification processes to re-extract his Radium. He had wanted to save this test for Mr. Toews, to dazzle him with the most striking possible demonstration of his success. But he had no choice. He had to know if he had succeeded. With a spoon he scraped the crystals from the hanger into various jars and glasses, then dissolved them in Sulphuric acid. He then added Zinc Sulphide, a phosphor that would convert the Radium's invisible radioactivity into visible light.

As a final, vital step, Adam added a few drops of colloidal silver. He had precious little of this chemical left, the rest having been confiscated after the greatest blunder of his career.

Besides disinterested teachers and rote schoolwork, Adam's greatest bane was Robbie Smulders, a nasty pimple of a boy responsible for a great many bruises and tears. There was no fighting or reasoning with him, for he was—as Adam had overheard Robbie's social worker mutter—incorrigible, a word Adam had found to mean 'incapable of changing'. Adam had thus sought to mark Robbie for life, to warn others of this hulking, cretinous waste of space. His agent of choice was colloidal silver, which, if ingested, would permanently stain Robbie's skin dark purple. But Adam was a scientist, not a secret agent, and his attempt to spike Robbie's food had been less than graceful. During the aftermath, Adam had felt true anxiety for the first time—anxiety over the fact that he, not Robbie, had faced expulsion. He, with his near-perfect marks and aptitude for science—and not that cruel delinquent. After that, Adam learned to take the abuse and keep a low profile. His research was far too important to compromise.

His solutions mixed, Adam rose and arranged the jars around the cramped shed. He kept his eyes half-closed, navigating by vague light and shadow; he did not wish to ruin the effect he sought. His task accomplished, he stood still in the centre of the musty room, eyes closed. Like Schrodinger's cat, both alive and dead until observed, the outcome of his year of dogged work hinged on the mere flicker of his eyelids. He stood poised on the cusp of absolute triumph or dismal failure.

He opened his eyes.

Adam seemed to enter a new new dimension. The jars of Radium bathed the room in an ethereal, crystal blue light. Adam seemed to float in this ghostly glow; it flowed through him, permeating his body. He smiled until the corners of his mouth could stretch no more. While others might have marveled at the mere beauty of this spectacle, Adam saw further still into its true wonder. All around him, trillions of atoms were disintegrating, hurling fragments of themselves into space in a manic bid for stability. He could see the swarm of nanoscopic Alpha and Beta particles streaking through the air around him, smashing into the molecules of phosphor floating in the jars. He saw the electrons jumping orbitals, firing off the blue photons coursing towards his eyes. Adam laughed as he thought of radioactive material in movies and TV shows, incongruously glowing bright green. Radioactivity, he knew, was invisible, requiring a phosphor to reveal its energy. Certain elements like Uranium glowed when immersed in water, but this Cherenkov Radiation was blue, not green. Adam grinned ear to ear: this torrent of knowledge spilling forth was intoxicating. Such knowledge infused everything around him with a sense of wonder, adding colour and depth to a sometimes flat, dull world. Upon seeing a badly-tuned TV, it always made him smile to consider that 1% of the crackling static was background radiation left over from the Big Bang. He had once pointed this out to his Mom when the TV had broken during her soaps, adding wryly that she could watch the birth of the universe.

"Stop talking nonsense", she had snapped. "If you're so smart, why don't you fix the goddamn TV? "

More than the mere joy of knowing, however, Adam felt the sheer ecstasy of understanding, the vindication of being right. Anyone could memorize and regurgitate a fact or principle, but applying said principle and making it real—making nature do one's bidding—was another matter entirely. It was the greatest possible confirmation of one's knowledge and mastery. Adam felt as though he were filled with Radium, the surging power and potential within him bursting forth in shining rays. It was a power beyond Robbie Smulders's painful punches or stinging taunts, a power beyond the mere physical. The infinite power of the mind.

Suddenly, Adam felt a tinge of sadness, disappointment at being unable to share this moment. If Mom and Dad were present, they would stare blankly at the blue glow, seeing everything but grasping nothing. They would nod indifferently, make some irrelevant comment about how pretty the light was, then depart unenlightened. They could not appreciate what Adam had accomplished; nor, Adam reflected, did he really want them to. At the first mention of 'radioactive', they would panic. The laboratory equipment would be hastily discarded, and Adam confined to his room indefinitely. It pained Adam to think of the boundless wonders their indifference blinded them to, the rich tapestry of knowledge they glossed over with dull trivialities. Mom worked in a hospital, but never spoke of medicine or biology. She merely reiterated how much she hated her coworkers, especially doctors. Dad worked in a factory but spoke passionately not of machines, but of unions and 'fat cats'.

Forget it, he thought, fixing his gaze once more upon the glowing jars before him. You'll soon be out of here. It was the fate of every child to wait, to serve out their time in school like a prison sentence until the far-off age of 18. But Adam's accomplishment would be his Get-Out-of-Jail card, the springboard that would propel his meteoric rise. He would win science fairs, acquire scholarships, and attend the finest schools in the world. A vision flashed through his mind: a vision of himself in an office many years from now, degrees and scientific awards hanging above his desk, a lifetime of discovery and achievement behind him. Remembering a quotation from Bill Gates—be nice to nerds; chances are you'll end up working for one—he imagined, with a cruel grin, all those who had in the past doubted or opposed him, fetching his coffee or cleaning his labware. This was his destiny, his future trajectory set in stone. He imagined this was how Marie and Pierre had lived out their final years, respected and lauded, her two Nobel prizes framed on the wall. He did not know for sure; he would have to find a complete biography.

"Adam. Dinner."

Adam barely heard Mom's flat, emotionless call from the back door, more a dejected sigh than an announcement. The triumphant joy within him drained away at once, as from a flask cracked by the heat of a Bunsen burner. Though he knew Mom would never walk the 50 feet necessary to discover his secret, Adam nonetheless packed away his equipment. Within minutes his entire laboratory lay safely concealed beneath the dust and rusty garden implements. Only the books above the potting bench staked his claim to this space. He bid adieu to his inner sanctum and the three hours of pure joy it had just afforded him, shuddering at the thought of the tasteless casserole and hour of pointless small talk that awaited him. Sighing, he gripped the door handle and strained against the stubborn slab of warped wood.

He winced, his fingers suddenly burning with pain. Withdrawing his hand, he held it up to the window's fading light. A large blister bulged from each fingertip. He frowned: where had these come from? He had not touched a Bunsen burner nor any other hot object. Or perhaps he had, but in his excitement had not noticed it. The burns were minor anyway; nothing to worry about. Shrugging, he forced the door open and emerged into a lilac twilight in the tangled garden. His success, he mused, had also opened a tenacious door. The dark wilderness of the unknown now laying before him, waiting to be conquered. Perhaps next he would extract Polonium, Thorium, or even Uranium. With a powerful enough ion source, he could generate neutrons and transmute elements—the ancient goal of the Alchemists. The possibilities were endless. Suddenly lifted by this thought, Adam marched triumphantly back to the house. Madame Curie would be proud, he thought.

… … …

Nuclear weapons are intrinsically neither moral nor immoral, though they are more prone to immoral use than most weapons.

—Herman Kahn

Mosaic G2 nuclear test, Montebello Islands, Australia, June 19, 1956.
nuclearweaponarchive.org/Uk/UKTesting.html

The Downwinders

AHARD RAIN FELL on Brisbane. Luke van Houdt sighed. At last, some relief from the scorching Australian summer. Luke was fond of rain; it reminded him of home back in The Hague. There was nothing better for a day's work than that soothing patter in the background. But today not even the rain could calm Luke's nerves. He was far behind schedule. On the workbench before him, amid a clutter of wires and screwdrivers, lay a yellow tinplate box with a curved handle, like a clothes iron. A large dial on its lid displayed radiation count. It was a Geiger counter, one of 20 he was to refurbish for the Air Force that day. With the turn of a screwdriver, he sealed in the device's complex electronic innards. Glancing at the clock, he cringed: only an hour remained before the client arrived to collect this batch. If he worked flat out, without interruption, he could just make the deadline.

Luke groaned as he heard the heavy creaks of Mr. Marston, the repair shop owner, lumbering up the stairs. Soon the obese figure of the man appeared in the doorway, wheezing from exertion. Luke averted his eyes.

"Boy!" Marston bellowed, in a voice like some brass instrument beaten within inches of its life. "You got that batch finished?"

"Almost, Mr. Marston," said Luke quickly. "Just on the last one. Then I can start calibration."

"What?" snapped Marston. "I said three o'clock! Air Force blokes'll be here in an hour!"

"Sorry, Mr. Marston," said Luke. "I'll have them done."

"Bloody cloggie," spat Marston, snorting in disgust. "What the hell'd I hire you for anyway?"

Luke said nothing.

"Get 'em done," Marston hissed, wagging a great sausage of a finger. "Or you're done. Got it, boy?"

"Yes, Mr. Marston."

"And take down that bloody billy," said Marston, pointing to the kettle filling in the rain on the windowsill. "I don't want a bloody suit if that falls on someone's head!"

With that, Marston turned and lumbered back down to the shop.

Luke sighed and rose from his seat. He needed something to calm his nerves. He hadn't any cigarettes left; tea would have to do. As Luke retrieved his kettle from the sill, he gazed out into the gunmetal gloom shrouding the city. The tall neon letters of MARSTON'S flashed garishly outside the window. What was he doing here, he wondered? Australia had once seemed a land of opportunity, a booming frontier far from a war-ravaged Europe. His reality, however, was this dismal workshop: a cluttered, dirty attic devoid even the luxury of running water. The sink in the corner had been clogged for months, and Marston was too cheap to have it repaired.

No time for such musings, Luke thought as he tossed the kettle onto his tiny gas stove. Almost as an afterthought, he switched on the radio—perhaps some music would help productivity. As the tubes warmed up, Luke dove straight back into his work. It seemed all he did these days was repair Geiger Counters. Demand had spiked as a result of all the atomic bombs the Brits were testing around the continent. Well-practiced, Luke operated on auto-pilot, stripping down the last Geiger counter. In rapid succession each component was expertly inspected, cleaned or replaced. When at last Luke screwed the tinplate cover home, fifteen minutes had elapsed. A half hour remained to calibrate the entire batch. Plenty of time, Luke assured himself. As if on cue, the kettle began to whistle. As Luke snatched it from the stove, the radio sprang to life.

"… that was Big Walkabout by Graeme Bell. This is Radio Melbourne at 3:30 in the afternoon on this the 26th of June, 1956. Here is the news…"

Luke reached across his workbench and slid over the 'Pig', the heavy cast-lead canister that held his calibration sources. Reaching in with tongs, he withdrew a small pellet of Cobalt-60. The radioactivity of this isotope was known, allowing him to easily check and calibrate the Geiger counters. Luke brandished the first of the devices, advancing the detector tube towards the source. It immediately burst into its characteristic rapid-fire chatter, the indicator needle swinging up the dial. Luke waited several seconds for the reading to stabilize.

"The British Royal Atomic Safety Commission announced today that last week's nuclear test in the Montebello Islands was a complete success. The test, codenamed Mosaic G1, was intended…"

120 Curies.

Strange, thought Luke: the dial should have read exactly 110. He withdrew the Geiger counter and approached the source anew. It again read 120. A less experienced technician might have dismissed the discrepancy as mere instrument error, but Luke knew better. He did a quick mental calculation: 120 Curies was equivalent to a typical chest x-ray every minute—far outside the acceptable tolerance range. Luke cursed: this would take far longer than expected. Reaching above his workbench, he pulled down his reference counter, which was recalibrated every day. He swept it over the source.

"…the test proved the efficiency of new weapons design technology that will be added to Britain's nuclear arsenal, allowing her to better defend herself…"

Luke did a double take. The reference counter read 120.

This can't be. I calibrated the damn thing this morning! Luke swept the source again, and again. The dial remained stubbornly drawn to 120. Replacing the detection tube had no effect. Casting the reference counter aside, he pulled up one of the refurbished units. It also read 120, as did the next, and the next. Luke frantically made his way through the entire batch, but to no avail. He slammed his fists on the workbench in frustration.

Calm down Luke, he thought, taking a deep breath. Think it through. The units could not be defective; what were the odds they would all read the same error? The error, he reasoned, must lie outside the Geiger counters. Perhaps the source was contaminated? Testing this theory, Luke retrieved another Cobalt pellet from the Pig and swept it with the reference counter.

"…Commission Chair Sir Ernest Titterton reported that, as predicted, the winds carried the fallout from the test safely out over the ocean. He foresees no ill effects for people…"

The dial read 120.

"What is going on!?" Luke exclaimed, trembling with frustration. Panic was setting in; Marston would have his hide if he didn't clear this up. Taking another deep breath, Luke poured himself a cup of tea and tried once more to reason through the problem. Radioactive decay did not simply increase overnight; something else had to be giving off the excess radioactivity. Perhaps another technician had lost a Cobalt source amid the clutter of the workshop. Yes, that must be it, he thought. Luke rose and brandished his reference counter again. Creeping slowly through the workshop, he swept the detector over every nook and cranny, hunting the errant source like a hog seeking truffles. But his instrument remained stubbornly silent, relaying only the intermittent pops and clicks of ordinary background radiation.

"…the Commission also announced that it will proceed with the construction of a permanent nuclear testing site at Maralinga in the Southern Province. Prime Minister Menzies called the plan a landmark in a new era of Anglo-Australian cooperation…"

Luke shut off the radio. The workshop was silent but for the soft rattle of the rain outside. Luke strained his ears as he swept the workshop anew, listening for the faintest chatter of radiation. He found nothing. Defeated, Luke slumped down in his chair. It was three o'clock: his time had run out. What was he to do? Though he was certain the Geiger counters were not in error, doubt still gnawed at his mind. What if he was wrong? What if the Air Force found the units defective? After all, this rogue radiation source had precluded proper calibration—they all read 120. What if he had made a mistake? He knew the answer, of course: Marston would kick him out on the street, and not figuratively at that. Luke pondered showing Marston the phantom radiation, proving the units were sound. No, it would only set him off.

Suddenly, Luke froze. The Geiger counter had begun chattering. Luke lunged for the detector and frantically dug through the clutter of his workbench. The reading tapered away to nothing. Luke sighed and leaned back into his chair.

The count spiked again.

What in the…

Glancing down, Luke realized that the Geiger counter was hovering over his teacup. Curious, he slowly lowered the instrument, immersing it in the tea. The device chattered loudly, the dial jumping to 120 Curies.

The tea? thought Luke, sweeping the Geiger counter over the kettle. It, too, was radioactive. He snatched his packet of tea leaves from the shelf and scanned it as well, but, strangely, it emitted no radiation. Luke frowned: if the tea leaves weren't the source, what then?

Luke felt a chill run down his spine. He slowly turned to face the open window.

It can't be…

With great trepidation, Luke slowly crept towards the window, Geiger counter held in his outstretched hand. The chatter steadily grew in intensity as he advanced, the needle creeping up the dial. Swallowing hard, he parted the blinds with his fingers and extended the detector out into the rain.

The count rose to 120 Curies.

Luke recoiled. There was no other explanation, no other conclusion he could draw.

The rain was radioactive.

Luke hastily shut the window. He stood there, paralyzed, for several long moments. His head swam. There was nothing else to do. He turned and clattered down the stairs.

Luke found Marston fast asleep behind the counter, his great gut rising and falling like a bellows with each wheezing snore. As Luke approached, he felt as one about to prod a hibernating bear. The outcome would be similar, he thought grimly, but this was too important to ignore.

"Mr. Marston," he whispered, prodding his shoulder.

"Hmmph…?" Marston grunted. "…hell do you want?"

"Mr. Marston, there's something I think you should see."

Marston snorted and sat up. "This had better be important, boy," he growled.

"It is, Mr. Marston. Come with…"

The doorbell chimed. Two Air Force officers in blue raincoats stepped into the shop, doffing their peaked caps in unison.

"Good afternoon," said one. "Are you Mr. Marston?" He had the breezy, nasal voice of a British aristocrat.

"Good afternoon, gentlemen," said Marston, turning away from Luke. He spread his arms, donning a broad, warm smile for the guests. "I expect you're here for the Geiger counters."

"Indeed," said one of the officers. "Are they ready?"

Marston glanced at Luke. "Well..?"

Luke needed no further prompting. He dashed up the stairs and returned with the full batch of Geiger counters, lining them up on the counter for inspection. Once finished, he stood silently in the corner as one of the officers examined his work.

"Yes," he muttered. "Yes, these will do quite nicely."

"We aim to please," Marston beamed. "Anything for the boys in blue, I always say."

"Could we have them carried to the car?" said the officer, inclining his head towards the blue Air Force sedan idling outside.

"Boy," said Marston simply. Luke obediently sprang forward and began packing the Geiger counters into a box. Suddenly he paused. He could take it no longer.

"Excuse me, gentlemen," he said, turning to the officers. "But there is something you should see. The rain… it is radioactive."

The officers cocked their heads.

"What is he talking about?" one asked Marston.

"No idea, sir," said Marston dismissively. "Don't mind him; fresh off the boat, he is. Hasn't learned to respect his superiors."

"Please, gentlemen," Luke insisted. "What I say is true. The rain outside—it is giving off 120 Curies. I measured it myself."

The officers flashed a curious glance at each other. One of them turned to Marston. "Might we have a word with him?"

"Be my guest," said Marston, sighing.

The officers turned to Luke.

"Shall we go up to your office?" said one, pointing upstairs.

"Well, I -"

"Splendid." The officers stepped forward in unison, herding Luke up the stairs. As he climbed, step by step, Luke felt as a condemned man being lead to the gallows. Reaching the workshop, the officers pulled two chairs over to Luke's workbench.

"Please, take a seat," said one, gesturing to Luke's chair. The officers removed their blue Macintosh coats, revealing their crisp khaki uniforms. Amid the multicoloured confetti of rank bars and winged insignia adorning their chests, Luke spotted two small black name tags: Lt. Sykes and Lt. Fosbery. They could have been twins, both with close-cropped sandy hair and probing grey eyes. Only Sykes's thin moustache differentiated them. They moved with eerie synchronicity, perfectly mirroring each other's movements. They stared silently at Luke, hands folded, as he sat down before them.

"Right," said Sykes. "What seems to be the problem, Mr…"

"van Houdt, sir," said Luke. "Luke van Houdt."

"Where are you from, Mr. van Houdt?" asked Fosbery.

"Nederland, sir. The Hague."

"Lovely country," said Sykes wistfully.

Luke forced a smile.

"Anyway," said Fosbery. "What seems to be the trouble?"

Luke shivered as their twin, piercing gazes fell on him. The interrogation had begun. He made to speak, but stopped. Instead, he simply placed his kettle before him and swept it with a Geiger counter. The harsh chattering cut through the strained silence like a bomb blast. After several long moments, Luke set the Geiger counter aside and folded his hands in his lap.

"That is rainwater," he said simply. "Collected today."

The officers were silent for many long moments, staring at the kettle with furrowed brows. Then, as if on some silent signal, they both produced cigarettes and lit them in perfect unison.

"Hmm…" said Sykes, surveying the kettle and Geiger counter laid on the desk. "No, I shouldn't worry about that."

"What?" said Luke.

"Nothing to be concerned about," Sykes explained casually. "There's radioactivity everywhere. Quite common, you know."

"Gentlemen…" said Luke slowly. "I am aware of background radiation, but this…this is 120 Curies. That is six chest x-rays per minute. You do realize this, yes?"

"Oh of course," said Fosbery. "We don't doubt you at all."

"But Science marches on, don't you know?" added Sykes. "Our research shows that levels like these are perfectly harmless."

"In fact," said Fosbery. "It seems a little radiation is good for you. Keeps things up and running, like a vaccine, you know?"

"So you see, it's nothing to be concerned about."

Both smiled disarmingly at Luke, awaiting his assent. Luke slowly shook his head, dumbfounded.

"Gentlemen, please understand. I am educated in nuclear physics: I graduated from The Hague University in 1947…"

"Oh, I don't doubt it, old boy," interrupted Fosbery. "But you don't have all the data we have. Top Secret, you know."

"We appreciate your concern, Mr. van Houdt," said Sykes. "Goodness knows we need more people like you. But rest assured there is nothing to be worried about."

Luke stared blankly at the officers. He no longer felt as though he were being interrogated. It was a psychoanalytic interview, with Luke the mental patient under the scrutiny of uniformed psychiatrists. They smirked amusedly at the curious specimen before them.

"I understand," said Luke. "Please, gentlemen, will you have some tea?" He held out the kettle.

The officers flashed a nervous glance at one other.

"No thank you," said Sykes. "We're on duty."

Luke lowered the kettle.

"It's the Montebello bomb, isn't it?" he said quietly.

"No," Sykes snapped. "Quite impossible."

"Then what?"

Fosbery shrugged. "An American test in the Pacific, I should imagine. Still, nothing to worry about."

"Still," said Sykes, recovering his casual smile "I don't think this needs to leave the room."

"No," Fosbery agreed. "After all, the people don't know all the facts that we do. Something like this…they might misunderstand."

"No sense in starting a needless panic, is there?" said Sykes.

Luke said nothing.

"So, Mr. van Houdt," said Fosbery. "We're placing you under the Official Secrets Act. Just to be safe."

"You are not to discuss this with anyone, do you understand?"

"It's best for everyone."

There was a long pause.

"Splendid," said Sykes with a broad smile. The officers rose simultaneously from their seats. "Glad that's settled. Now, Mr. van Houdt, we'll leave you to your work."

Luke remained at his workbench, wordless as he stared vacantly at the scratches and burns in the wood. The officers donned their coats and marched in step down the stairs.

Outside there was a flash. Thunder rolled over Brisbane. Nothing in life is to be feared, it is only to be understood.

... ...

Now is the time to understand more so that we may fear less.

—Marie Curie

The first person to receive linear accelerator therapy for retinoblastoma, being treated in 1957.
en.wikipedia.org/wiki/File: External_beam_radiotherapy_retinoblastoma_nci-vol-1924-300.jpg

A is for Atom

ANNE MULLIGAN scaled the bulldozer standing derelict before the gates, rising high above the crowd. As she climbed, the ragged congregation cheered, pumping their fists and waving hand-painted signs in the cold autumn air. Frenzied applause erupted as Anne climbed atop the cab, arms raised in triumph. Silhouetted behind her in the gray morning haze stood the skeletal frame of the half-finished turbine hall. As Anne slowly lowered her arms, the cheers tapered to silence. She paused for effect, surveying her disciples gathered below.

"My friends!" she cried. "The time has come for us to send a message. That we refuse to remain voiceless! That our health and that of our children will no longer be at the mercy of greedy corporations who poison our earth! That we decide what is best for us, not some scientists in a lab!"

Convulsively, Anne lurched and gesticulated, locked in some violent trance. Her diatribe twisted her face into a grotesque mask of gnashing teeth and fiery eyes.

"The chief engineer for this power plant," she said, gesturing to the unfinished building behind her. "has assured me there is nothing to fear. That this is a "next generation" reactor and cannot possibly fail. But is that not what they always say? Do they not always say there is nothing to fear, that the scientists and engineers have it all under control? And are they not always wrong? After Three Mile Island was Chernobyl! After that, Fukushima! Enough is enough! We can no longer stand for this height of human hubris!"

Olivia Masters turned away from the television in disgust. Stepping into the hospital corridor, she pulled out her cell phone and dialed her brother. Back in the technicians" lounge, the news broadcast cut back to the anchors.

"Hello?" her brother answered.

"Hi, Charlie," said Olivia. "Just wanted to see how everything was going."

"More of the same," Charlie sighed. "The head brass and politicians are still negotiating. Hopefully they'll finally send the cops and clear these jokers out."

"Here's hoping," said Olivia. "Oh!" she added, pulling a business card from her scrubs pocket. "I found another company that's hiring: K&B. They're building the new mall downtown."

"Thanks, sis," said Charlie wearily. "I'll check them out."

"Okay, I have to go now. Love you."

Olivia hung up and grunted in frustration. Poor Charlie, she thought. He had been so sure things were finally turning around. The day Stockton Construction was awarded the Pine Woods contract had been his happiest in a while. That was, of course, until 'Atomic Annie' and her gang arrived. The building crews had been barred from the site for two weeks now. As far as Olivia was concerned, the police should have kicked out those tree-huggers the minute they arrived. But with the project already unpopular, the company had opted to negotiate rather than risk further controversy.

Through glass doors, Olivia entered the oncology department. Unlike the sterile hospital corridors, the rooms here were more invitingly appointed: potted plants stood in the corners; art prints hung on the walls. Strange as it seemed, such touches made all the difference for those facing slow, wasting death. Guttering out like a candle in the emergency room, one had little time to notice the decor.

Past the waiting room Olivia entered the Chemotherapy lounge, where a dozen patients sat quietly in plush armchairs. Some wore wigs or bandannas; others bravely showcased their bald heads. All were tethered to small bags of chemicals hanging above their heads like balloons, the life preservers keeping them afloat. Olivia smiled warmly as she passed through, approaching an even greater wonder.

Entering a small room crammed with computer screens, she gazed through a large lead-glass window and beheld the radiotherapy machine. It was a formidable device, a gleaming chrome cylinder hanging from a massive robotic arm. It looked like something from science fiction; no: it was science fiction. For this futuristic ray gun could erase tumors. The specifics were more complex than that, of course, but Olivia never lost sight of this simple truth. It was nothing short of miraculous.

"Good morning," said a voice. "Or… is it afternoon? I've lost track."

Rick, a fellow technician, was sitting in the corner. His eyes were bloodshot, his hair disheveled.

"It's morning," said Olivia. "Go home: you look like hell."

Rick shook his head. "Can't. Gotta make up for that week I took off around Christmas."

"How long you been up for?"

"Going on twenty-six hours," said Rick wearily, downing the last cold dregs of his coffee. "And I got ten sessions left. Go figure, huh?" He gestured to a large stack of medical charts on the desk.

"I'll take a few off your hands," said Olivia, flipping through the charts. "Make your day a little…"

She stopped mid-sentence, staring in disbelief at the paper in her hands.

No. It can't be…

"Uh…give me a minute, will you?" she said, springing to her feet. Leaving without another word, she raced back to the waiting room. She opened the door and surveyed the anxious faces within.

Her jaw dropped.

You have got to be kidding me…

"What the hell was that about?" said Rick as Olivia returned. "You sure you're okay?"

"Uh-huh," said Olivia absently. "Say, Rick: why don't I take over for you today?"

"Thanks," Rick yawned. "But I can't. Like I said, I gotta…"

"You shouldn't be working when you're this tired," Olivia commanded, pulling Rick to his feet and hustling him out the door. "Go home, get some sleep, come back tomorrow. Got it?"

"Yes ma'am," said Rick, mock-saluting her. "Thanks a million, okay?" he added, smiling wearily.

Olivia nodded and shut the door behind him. She then returned to her station and began calibrating the machine. Her hands trembled; she could barely type. Mustering her discipline, she forced herself through the procedure with her usual thoroughness. Her patience was finally rewarded as her first patient shuffled into the therapy room.

Olivia couldn't believe her eyes. There, draped in a paper hospital gown, was Anne Mulligan.

Olivia suppressed a smirk. The irony was delicious: here was the nuclear industry's Public Enemy Number One, about to undergo radiation therapy. You can't make this up, she thought.

"Hello?" said Anne, tapping her foot impatiently. "Can we get this over with, please?"

"Just a minute," said Olivia, forcing a smile as she entered the therapy room. She avoided eye contact, carrying out her duties in a perfunctory manner.

"Take off your gown, lie down," she said. Anne gave an indignant glare, but obeyed. Olivia glanced at her naked, vulnerable body. Not so intimidating now, are you? she thought. Anne's chest had been tattooed with a cruciform pattern to align the radiation beam: the perfect mark for a self-styled martyr.

"Lie perfectly still," said Olivia, retreating to the control room.

The machine hummed to life, swinging ominously over Anne Mulligan like some great beast sniffing its quarry. Anne fidgeted on the table, once-fiery eyes now wide with nervous apprehension, as Olivia aligned the laser crosshairs with the tattoos, targeting the grape-sized tumor in Anne's left lung. Precision was everything: an error of millimeters could turn the radiation beam from cure to killer.

Olivia still could not believe it: here was the woman behind Charlie's troubles, that spiteful, irrational woman hell-bent on destroying an industry that brought clean energy, jobs and medical miracles to so many. Olivia wanted to storm into that room, unleash all her frustration and bile. But, as a professional, she could only speak to patients about the procedure. Anne was in her sights, yet Olivia was powerless.

Unless…

Olivia's hands seemed to move of their own accord, as though she had slipped into a trance. With the alignment camera she snapped dozens of photographs of Anne on the table, summarily consigning them to her flash drive. Olivia then began gathering Anne's medical charts.

"Is it starting?" said Anne, voice tremulous.

"Uh, sorry for the delay," said Olivia. "I just have to consult with a doctor. Stay right there."

Olivia ducked out, briskly striding to the nearest copy room. Frantically she ran off the charts, glancing nervously behind her lest someone walk in. Mercifully, she was alone. Hurrying back to the control room, Olivia hastily stuffed the copies in her purse and breathed a sigh of relief.

I have you now, she thought, allowing herself a satisfied smirk.

"Are you finished "consulting"?" said Anne, now off the table and pacing the room. "Can we please get on with this?"

Olivia took a deep breath and composed herself. She could now continue the procedure as with any other patient. With her evidence safely stowed, Olivia could deal with Anne later.

"Lie back down, please," said Olivia flatly.

"How long will this take?" Anne griped. "I have an important appointment."

"Oh, where do you need to be?"

"I don't think that's any of your business," Anne snapped.

Olivia froze. The adrenaline rush of her photocopying spree had worn off. She glanced nervously to the control room, where the incriminating documents lay tucked in her purse. Her mind reeled, recoiling at what she had done. What had she been thinking? Never could she have imagined herself so blatantly violating doctor-patient confidentiality. She could lose her job. Nor could she have imagined herself laughing at another's misfortune—let alone exploiting it. Anne was still a patient, suffering from the great sorrow that Olivia knew all too well. Yet this schadenfreude could not be helped. What else could one feel for someone who railed against science and technology while blissfully reaping its benefits? Despite the alarm bells ringing in her head, Olivia could not ignore this opportunity. She could finally discredit Anne Mulligan; ruin her forever. The chance would never come again. Yet no matter how much she hated this woman—or loved Charlie—she could not justify blackmail. Perhaps she could just walk out; after all, why should she treat such an ungrateful hypocrite? But if she didn't treat Anne, someone else would.

There has to be another way…

"Sorry, it's just you look very familiar," Olivia recovered. "Wait: aren't you that activist?" she added.

Anne nodded.

"I thought so. Just saw you on TV. Pine Woods, right?"

"Well, it's good to know the word is getting out," said Anne, her voice now bright and flighty as a kindergarten teacher's. "Hopefully it will bring more people to the cause."

"Just what are you protesting?" said Olivia, acting dumb. "I thought we needed a new power plant."

Anne gave Olivia a pained, patronizing expression, a face for small children. "Oh dear," she cooed. "You're one of those people who believe the engineers and politicians, aren't you?"

Olivia twitched.

"I wish I could say I was surprised," Anne continued. "They probably drilled all sorts of nonsense into you in school. But believe me: they lie. They always lie."

"Oh?"

"Well, they probably told you that nuclear power is 'clean'", Anne explained. "But of course they never showed you the 300 million tons of nuclear garbage littering this country. They say they have it all under control, but really they have no idea what to do with it. And they don't care: all they want is more electricity and profits. And people wonder why cancer rates are going up; just look at me…"

Olivia glanced at Anne's yellow-stained fingers. Was everything this woman said a lie? Olivia knew more than most about nuclear power thanks to Charlie: he had done research on the industry before signing on to Pine Woods. Olivia knew of the 300 million tons of waste, and that it remained unburied because of people like Anne protesting permanent repositories. She also knew that cancer rates were rising, but only because life expectancy was increasing. In the past, few lived long enough to die of cancer. If Anne had done her research, she would have known. Why those without science education felt they could comment on scientific matters was beyond Olivia.

"I'm sure they'll figure something out," said Olivia, still playing the fool. "Aren't they building some repository in Nevada?"

"They always have 'plans', dear," said Anne. "They didn't do a lot of good for my Bobby."

Olivia hesitated. Bobby Mulligan was Anne's son. Five years ago a storage tank at the old West Valley nuclear reprocessing facility had leaked into a stream where Bobby was swimming. His subsequent battle with leukemia had been press fodder for months, and from his death emerged the Anne Mulligan everyone knew. It was a tragic story, and Olivia certainly sympathized. A mother's grief was a terrible thing. But that, she realized, was Anne's intention. Bobby Mulligan was the poster child of the anti-nuclear movement, their perpetual sympathy card. In every debate and interview, the mere mention of his name could trip the most cynical tongues.

"I'm sorry for your loss," said Olivia, adopting a soft, disarming voice reserved for skittish patients. "But accidents happen with all technologies. Cars and planes kill more people than reactors."

"Everyone says that," said Anne dismissively. "But can a car accident contaminate the environment for thousands of years? Does a plane crash poison people halfway across the globe?"

"Well, no technology is perfected overnight," said Olivia, struggling to hide the contempt in her voice.

"You keep believing that," Anne chuckled, glancing at the machine overhead. "But if you want my advice, dear: change careers. There are things humanity just wasn't meant to tamper with."

"Then why don't you just die?" Olivia muttered under her breath.

"What was that?"

"Nothing," Olivia deflected.

Anne suddenly sat bolt upright, staring Olivia straight in the eyes. "If you have something to say to me," she said tersely. "Say it. If there's something I can't abide, it's a coward."

"Well look who's talking," Olivia shot back.

"I beg your pardon?"

Olivia had gone too far. She glanced again to her purse, its sensitive cargo now worthless. If she released those records now, Anne would know it was her. There was no backing down now, no graceful retreat. Whatever Olivia said now, Anne would report. All she could do was seize this opportunity, go down in a blaze of glory.

"If you want my opinion, Mrs. Mulligan," said Olivia, glaring at Anne. "You're nothing but a hypocrite."

Olivia felt a great knot within her suddenly release. How long she had waited for someone to call Anne out to her face. She braced for the fiery, whirlwind reaction.

But Anne seemed completely unfazed. "Really?" she said simply. "How so?"

Olivia's jaw dropped. "How so?" she exclaimed. "How about you, of all people, electing for radiation therapy? Don't you see a problem here? Doesn't it bother you?"

Anne shrugged. "I'm on a mission, and I fully intend on seeing it through to the end. Now I can't very well do that if I die, can I? Sacrifices always need to be made; the cause is greater than myself."

"Yes, I'm sure it's a great sacrifice to save yourself and deny others the privilege," spat Olivia. "Tell me: what happens if you 'see your mission through'? What then?"

"Then that abomination at Pine Woods doesn't get built," Anne replied with a smug smirk. "If I had my way, I'd tear them all down."

"And what happens to my patients?" said Olivia, trembling with frustration. "What do I tell them? 'Sorry, we can't treat your cancer. The reactor that makes our radioisotopes was torn down.'?"

"Once we get rid of nuclear power," Anne countered. "There won't be much cancer left to treat. Believe me, dear: I'm helping more people than you think. An ounce of prevention…"

Olivia could stand it no more. "I'm sorry!" she interrupted. "But you're just wrong! You get a higher radiation dose from coal soot than reactors, did you know that? You get a higher dose from potassium in bananas! And do you know what the most common cancers I see are? Lung, breast, bladder, colorectal…completely unrelated to radiation! Radiation saves people, Mrs. Mulligan!"

Anne remained unmoved, her expression calm. Facts seemed to simply bounce off her.

"Alright, to hell with it," Olivia finally exclaimed. "You want to help people, Mrs. Mulligan? Why don't you start by helping my brother: he's on the construction crew for Pine Woods. He's got a family and he's about to default on his mortgage because of you!"

Olivia panted heavily, quaking with rage as she glared at Anne.

"You're not a mother, are you?" Anne sighed. "I thought not. But say you lost your baby—or your brother his. Wouldn't you do anything to make sure they didn't die in vain?"

Olivia stared Anne straight in the eye. "Maybe," she said slowly. "But I think I'd eventually move on. You can't do anything for the dead. I'd keep helping the living. Those I can still help."

"Then go to it," said Anne, lying back down on the table.

Olivia stood stunned for several long moments. In a daze, she slowly backed away, retreating into the control room. As she had many times before, she re-aligned the machine and prepared to unleash its invisible double-edged blade, that treacherous but life-saving beam. If all went well, she knew, Anne Mulligan would walk out and return to her crusade. She would continue to mislead impressionable minds, to spread the cancer of irrationality and misguided anger. But Olivia would remain as well, here or wherever they would have her. While Anne stormed and raged, she would continue helping those in need the best way she knew how—by offering hope.
By performing small miracles daily.

Sign outside of the Uranium Enrichment site at Oak Ridge, Tennessee, 1945.
neutrontrail.com/2010/09/ dancing_physics_society_the_matter_of_origins/

Mercury Astronaut John Glenn training in a simulator, January 11, 1961
theatlantic.com/infocus/2011/02/the-historic-flight-of-mercury-6/100012/

Part III

Leaving

the

Cradle

"Fallen Astronaut" statuette and memorial plaque left on the moon by the crew of Apollo 15 on August 1, 1971
photosofwar.net/war-photos/fallen-astronaut/
["The Farest and Loneliest, yet, Greatest Memorial of the Solar System - Fallen Astronaut 1971" Photos of War, August 2012]

··· ··· ···

Don't tell me that man doesn't belong out there. Man belongs wherever he wants to go—and he'll do plenty well when he gets there.

—Wernher von Braun

From now on, we live in a world where man has walked on the moon. It wasn't a miracle, we just decided to go.

—Jim Lovell

The earth is the cradle of humanity, but one cannot live in a cradle forever.

—Konstantin Tsiokovsky

Astronauts Jim Lovell and Buzz Aldrin just prior to the Gemini XII mission, November 11, 1966.
images.ksc.nasa.gov/photos/1966/high/
[Photo 66C-9220; Kennedy Space Centre Archives]

Foreword: Into the Wild Blue Yonder

IT WAS A COOL JULY MORNING when I stood on a Florida beach, gazing up at the sky. Dark fingers of cloud loitered overhead, and a thick haze shrouded the horizon. When I awoke that morning, the sky was black. Torrential rain drummed on the hotel roof. Yet still I came, driving down dark, rainswept highways to the coast. Hopeful eyes watching the menacing skies. At last a faint salmon glow broke through the gloom, and my spirits were lifted. Those clouds had parted slowly, curtains drawn by a reluctant stagehand. The stage lay in the distance, beyond the sweeping crescent of sand. Through the haze I caught glimpses of a thin black line stretching out to sea, strange shapes of hangars, gantries, and cranes rising from its back. From here, behind the smoky veil, would emerge the greatest spectacle known to man. I had only to wait—and hope.

Thousands of fellow pilgrims lined the beach. Some played in the pounding surf, while others, on blankets and chairs strewn about the sand, fitfully read their paperbacks. But our restless minds were drawn to that line on the horizon, and to that unseen clock counting ever downwards. Apprehension hung like the sea haze.

At long last, silence fell. Like automatons at some unseen signal, we rose as one. We stood frozen in a surreal tableau, awed mannequins planted in the sand. Some pressed phones to their ears, listening. Some warily eyed the dark clouds waiting in the wings, poised to usurp the clear skies. Let it last, we prayed. Just a few minutes more. Please, let it last.

Then an excited murmur rumbled through the crowd, a trickle that became a torrent.

"Nine, eight, seven…"

All eyes were fixed, unblinking, on the horizon, beyond the terra-cotta ranks of beachfront hotels. We held our collective breath. The next precious few seconds would be the culmination of months of careful planning, days of frantic travel, and a lifetime of dreaming.

"Six, five, four…"

This was it. We were here! History was about to be made.

"Three, two, one…zero!"

The surf calmly lapped the sand. Palm fronds rustled in the sea breeze. Gulls wheeled lazily overhead. Frantic eyes scoured the horizon, but nothing stirred. We exchanged furtive, fearful glances. Had we missed it? What had happened? As the precious seconds slipped past, the awful stillness trickled into our hearts until, saturated, they sank. It was over: the loitering clouds had played their dirty trick. Dejectedly we shuffled away, sulking back to the surf or our blankets in the sand. We forced smiles, resigning ourselves to what was now an ordinary day at the beach.

But suddenly—incredibly—that excited murmur flashed anew down the beach. We sprang from our blankets, scrambled from the surf, and gathered once more in awestruck silence as one man, phone pressed to his ear, excitedly called out the countdown.

"Five, four, three, two, one…"

Thousands of outstretched arms saluted the bright new star that rose in the sky. The lashing tongue of flame rose on a roiling pillar of smoke, as if climbing a tower whose stones it frantically laid beneath its feet. Wide eyes and frantically-snapping cameras followed the fiery comet as it soared ever higher, streaking a graceful arc over the beach. Agape, we thought of the four brave souls perched atop that flaming geyser, blasting like a meteor into the heavens. Our spirits soared with them as we cheered them on their way.

"Go! Go! Go!"

It was over all too quickly. Soaring over the water, the shooting star arced high over the clouds. We caught brief glimpses as it darted between the pale furrows, but soon it was lost from view. Then a peal of thunder crashed down onto the beach as the craft punched through the sound barrier. This final salute reverberated through the crowd for a few final moments, then all was silent. Only the hulking column of smoke that loomed over the beach bore witness to that magic moment, come and gone. Soon the wind would sweep away this ephemeral monument, and the reluctant sky would yield to jealous rainclouds. But that night a new star would appear in the heavens, ferrying four human beings to their new home beyond the sky.

That was 11:29 AM on July 8, 2011 when the space shuttle Atlantis rose gracefully off its launch pad and departed on STS-135, its 33rd and final mission. The words above capture the wonder and majesty of being there on that historic day, as that wondrous creation of mankind hurtled off into the sky. Indeed, the enormity of what I had witnessed did not hit home until the next day, when I stood, awestruck, beneath the vast engine bells of the Saturn V rocket that once carried men to the moon. That this 3,000-ton skyscraper was made to actually fly spoke to a wonderful truth: man is truly capable of miracles. It is such wonders that made me become an engineer.

Thirteen days later, after a successful mission, Atlantis touched down on the Kennedy Space Centre runway. The squeal of its tires on the pavement marked the end of an era: after 30 years of triumph and tragedy, the Space Shuttle Program was over. The orbiters were shipped to museums, their launch pads razed to await a new generation of spacecraft. I did not mourn for the Shuttle; its time had come. As I cheered Atlantis on its twilight voyage, I looked to the future, and the possibilities that lay ahead. On December 8, 2010, not far from where Atlantis lifted off, the unmanned SpaceX Dragon capsule thundered off the launch pad aboard a Falcon 9 rocket, becoming the first privately-funded spacecraft to orbit the earth and successfully return. On May 25, 2012, Dragon successfully rendezvoused with the International Space Station. As of this writing, regular cargo flights are scheduled to begin in September 2013, kickstarting an exciting future of private spaceflight. Freed of the whims of shifting government budgets and priorities, who knows what leaps manned space exploration will take in years to come?

As a lifelong space enthusiast and engineering student, I have often had to answer cynics who see no value in manned space exploration. Why spend billions sending men into space, they say, when they could be spent on food, medicine and other aid for the impoverished of the world? I have also heard apologists appeal to man's innate 'drive to explore' or the many spinoff technologies—Mylar, microelectronics, Teflon, hydrogen fuel cells—that now benefit millions. But to appeal to man's nature is to indulge in an is-ought fallacy, and to defend space exploration by its unintended byproducts is to cynically miss the point. The power of manned space exploration lies not in the mundanely useful projects it happens to produce, but it its profound power to inspire us. How many children in the 1950s and 60s, watching the first satellites shoot off into the mysterious realm of outer space, were inspired to become engineers and scientists? And how many more after men themselves took that bold leap into the unknown? Manned space exploration captures the imagination like no satellite or deep-space probe can, for we can see ourselves taking the journey. We live vicariously through the astronauts, and in contributing to their missions—even by designing even the smallest screw on a spacecraft—we feel like we are up there with them, taking part in the adventure. Is this not a superior sentiment to that other great mother of invention: the desire to kill each other? Many technologies we use everyday—microwave ovens, sunscreen, Nylon—are the products of warfare, a crucible of creativity if ever there was one.

And as the horrors of communism have made all too clear, redistributing wealth for the benefit of all leads only to further decay and misery. It holds the best and brightest—and humanity as a whole—back. As astronaut Buzz Aldrin eloquently stated: "We can continue to try and clean up the gutters all over the world and spend all of our resources looking at just the dirty spots and trying to make them clean. Or we can lift our eyes up and look into the skies and move forward in an evolutionary way." After all, is the inspiration that makes a man improve his lot in life—to take control of his destiny—not worth more than the sack of grain that will idly sustain him for a few miserable days more? Our salvation lies in the stars, not the aid camp.

As with any bold new venture, there will always be missteps and tragedies, blind alleys and corruption. In the span of only 12 years, mankind went from being an earthbound species to walking on the moon. In mere decades, it seemed, we would be living on Mars and vacationing to the outer planets. But the cooling of Cold War and the end of the public's fickle honeymoon with space scuttled our futuristic ambitions, and we fell into decades of stagnation and pedestrian excursions into low earth orbit. And in the wake of both superpowers' scramble into space were the bodies of many brave astronauts, victims of haste and expediency. But the launch of Dragon and Falcon 9 turned a new page in the history of manned spaceflight, opening the sky to us all. As I did in the case of nuclear power in A is For Atom, in this collection, I have attempted to capture all facets of our journey into space: promise, corruption, and eventual redemption. Only one question remains: where to next? I have sat by night beside a cold lake

... ...

And touched things smoother than moonlight on still water, But the moon on this cloud sea is not human, And here is no shore, no intimacy, Only the start of space, the road to suns.

—F.R. Scott, 'Trans-Canada'

Major Joe Kittinger performing the record-breaking Excelsior III skydive, August 16, 1960.
en.wikipedia.org/wiki/File:Kittinger-jump.jpg

The Highest Step

THE WORLD was at his feet. Few could ever claim this literally. Yet as the jumper gazed through the thin circle of glass, he beheld the spectacle of the globe in its entirety spread out below him, his entire universe at a glance. How frail, how insubstantial it seemed from this vantage: a hollow ball of blown glass, glowing ethereal blue as if lit from within. From here he could perceive the full curvature of the globe, sweeping across the panorama of his vision. And between this majestic arc and the darkest blackness imaginable, he saw the thin band of glowing blue haze, no thicker than a coat of varnish painted upon a desk-top globe: the atmosphere, all that shielded the earth from the harsh universe beyond. So faint and ephemeral; it seemed he could sweep it away with a mere brush of his hand. He gazed up through the porthole at the gossamer envelope that towered over the gondola, all that kept him aloft. His craft sailed as a ship at sea, skimming across the vaporous spray atop a vast ocean of thin air. All the atmosphere lay beneath him: the spring rains, the summer breezes, the tempests and typhoons. He laid his hand upon the thin aluminium sphere of the gondola, all that protected him from the cold, hostile vacuum. Once free of this protective cocoon, his own armour would be frailer still: a few layers of cloth, rubber and plastic would be all that stood between him and the void, a thin, billowing shroud all that separated him from the fate of countless meteors that dared brave the planet's deceptively vaporous defences. He would carry his own atmosphere, a miniature earth that would accompany his long descent back home.

These things he knew as statements of fact, just as he knew his altitude: thirty-six kilometres above sea level, far loftier than the mightiest mountains. Yet this was mere data; he felt nothing, no visceral sense of where he now stood. This was a world beyond instinct, a place that strained the imagination to its breaking point. How inconceivable that certain death lay mere centimetres away, beyond the protective walls of the gondola. How unfathomable that at this altitude, it would take him a quarter hour to descend to the firm ground. Beyond a certain height—he could not say precisely when—a human being lost all perspective and scale. The addition of hundreds or thousands of metres did not matter; he may as well have been lying still upon the ground, the portholes mere television screens. He seemed to experience this world through a numbing wall of lead; only once outside the gondola would he truly understand the alien world he had ventured into. He could scarcely imagine the plight of his predecessor, crouching alone in an open gondola as he made his journey to the edge of space fifty years before.

Oddly, this strange sense of detachment proved a blessing, for the jumper could conduct his final preparations in peace, without fear or anxiety. As he donned his clear helmet, the loud hiss of oxygen drowned out all else, further isolating him from the world. Oh to venture out unclothed, he thought, to fully immerse himself in this exotic environment above the sky. But this was not the world of men, and such a venture would have been his last. Memories and discovery were of no use to a dead man.

The jumper was ready. Twisting a valve, he bled his artificial atmosphere into the vacuum outside. As the gondola depressurized, the jumper tapped his gloved hand rhythmically upon the aluminium walls, listening as the sound slowly faded away to nothingness. He was now in a silent world, a dead world. He unlatched the hatch, the last barrier between him and the unknown. As his portal swung away, he found himself face-to-face with the earth, 36 km directly below.

The cirrocumulus clouds that once soared high above now lay far below in a brilliant, glowing white sheet, undulating like ripples of sand on the shore. Between the gaps in these pearl dunes, the deepest valleys and tallest mountains were mere wrinkles and scratches in a smooth, mottled field. The jumper was reminded of azure waters and coral sands of a tropical sea; he felt as a diver in a diving bell, ready to plunge into the trenches and seamounts in a crystal abyss. The sun glinted from the body of an airliner skimming above the clouds, as far below him that it was above the ground. A sudden wave of trepidation washed over the jumper as he abruptly gained his once-elusive perspective. But he did not hesitate. Granting fear no purchase, he launched himself into the void.

Something was wrong. He must have become snagged, gotten caught on the gondola. For he was not falling. He was still, weightless, suspended in space. Yet as the jumper cast his gaze upwards, he beheld the shocking sight of the balloon and gondola rocketing skyward, accelerating away from him. But there was no air left to rise through; it was he who was falling from the balloon. Yet no wind ruffled his suit; no lace or strap stirred. The ploughed fields of cirrocumulus clouds below drew no closer. There was no air to mark his fall; only the balloon, which soon shrank to a faint white point and was lost amid the deep black sky.

Outside the bubble of the jumper's helmet, the world was spinning. His body tumbled like a bauble on a string, whirling through the silent sky as the thickening air clung to his suit. The jumper flexed and strained against the stiff inflated joints of his suit, struggling in vain to correct his wild gyrations. Why had his drogue not deployed? Without it, he would continue to spin, accelerating to a lethal rate as his blood pooled in his head. He would greet the earth as a lifeless mass, wrapped in his own shroud. The drogue should have deployed within ten seconds; he had already fallen for what seemed like many minutes. As the horizon smeared dizzyingly to a blue pastel blur, the jumper clawed frantically at his chest for the manual release. He felt as though mired in quicksand, his every movement ponderous and lethargic. His heartbeats blazed to a deafening whir as a wave of terror washed over him. A cold sweat flashed through his suit. Was this it? Was he to end here, dashed across the atmosphere?

Suddenly he felt the faint click near his shoulders and was jerked violently upwards as the tiny square of nylon deployed. He snapped from his violent spin, the hazy blue blur resolving to the crystal sphere. Winded by the deployment, the jumper fought to regain his breath. What had taken so long? He glanced at the altimeter on his wrist. Nothing had gone wrong. The drogue had deployed exactly on time. But the sheer, alien bombardment of new sensations had stretched mere seconds into an eternity. Now soaring smoothly high above the glowing vista, he could at last gaze upon the planet from the greatest stage on earth.

The broad swath of the Americas lay cloaked under the snowy drifts of cirrocumulus; he could spy only glimpses of the land below. He imagined a great cobbler or tailor, scattering swatches of odds-and-ends across the floor: the brilliant pearls and rhinestones of Greenland and the Arctic Archipelago, the dark, lush felt of the northern boreal forests and South American jungles. The burlap and sable of the Great Plains blending into the rusty leather and shagreen of fiery, sun-baked deserts. Across the broad, shimmering opal of the Atlantic, the craggy, herringbone shoreline of Norway could be seen, arcing down to the mottled green twill of mainland Europe. At the limits of the jumper's vision, the green-and-tan batik scarf of Africa disappeared behind the bowed horizon. He perceived no borders, nor other signs of his fellow species. Only in darkness, he mused when an electric blaze turned so many nights into day, would they be plainly seen. Only the isle of Hispaniola in the azure Caribbean directly below betrayed signs of humanity, its long mass bisected into lush green jungle and brown wasteland. From here, all life seemed but a minute film, clinging tenaciously to the surface like algae or lichen upon a great stone.

The jumper's suit began to ruffle and billow in the thickening atmosphere. The air had returned. The once-tiny ripples of the clouds had swelled into vast mountains, seemingly as solid as any terrestrial monolith. The jumper stretched his arms and legs behind him, diving headfirst at breakneck speed as the massive white folds swallowed him. His vision faded to a featureless, glowing grey haze. Millions of tiny ice crystals hissed as they impinged upon his clear plastic helmet. Such was his tremendous velocity that he sliced through these lofty clouds in mere moments. The world of sound had returned: the wind roared as it beat furiously upon his body. He was now a meteor, shuddering and buffeting as he careened earthward at the speed of sound. The continents and oceans opened beneath him, speckled and streaked with whorls, spirals and galaxies of clouds to rival the finest Van Gogh. The glaring sun blazed upon the mirrored surface of the waters; the jumper reached to his helmet and lowered his amber sunshade. On cue, another faint click and massive jerk signalled the release of his primary chute, which unfurled like some monstrous jellyfish above him. His body snapped upright as he floated through the wisps of clouds. His helmet fogged with moisture, which he clumsily wiped with a thickly gloved hand.

The snow-flecked peaks of the Sierras had sprung up in sharp relief beneath him, sandcastles on a grand, sweeping beach. The Great Salt Lake and Bonneville Flats sprawled as patches of crusty white lichen upon the hard, sun-baked deserts. The vast centipede of the Grand Canyon crawled across the rusty landscape to the south. Above, the clouds receded at a frightening pace; his precipitous descent was barely checked by the tiny nylon canopy. But as the scars and scratches of the ancient earth grew sharper and the sprawling, shimmering tendrils of cities began to emerge from the landscape, his gossamer companion detached automatically, crumpling and pulsating as it drifted away. The jumper felt his heart rise to his throat as he plummeted freely once more, his final canopy unfurling in a long billowing stream against him. At last his final life-preserving shroud snapped open and he floated silently on a high desert breeze. The vast curve of the earth had disappeared; the flat, stone-strewn billiard table of the desert floor stretched over every horizon. The jumper braced as the ground swept up to meet him, his knees crumpling on impact. He tumbled onto his back, at last reunited with the good earth. How strange it felt, this solid ground, now that he had plumbed an airless, weightless realm. The jumper removed his helmet, breathed the dry desert air. He felt the warm, dusty wind. The sunburst stretched its fiery arms across the sapphire blue through which he had just plummeted.

Some would call him an astronaut. But the jumper had no more claim to that title than a mariner to that of aeronaut. He had but sailed atop a vast ocean, timidly retreating to the safety of the protective terrestrial womb. The jumper had seen the infinite sky. He had glimpsed the new frontier, the greatest adventure known to mankind.

... ...

Russia is still the leader in world space exploration. But its position of leader involves great responsibility—we have no right to lag behind. We can and we must move constantly forward.

—Valentina Tereshkova

"In the Ocean of Storms", painting by Russian Cosmonaut Aleksey Leonov, 1967
en.wikipedia.org/wiki/Soviet_manned_lunar_programs

In The Ocean Of Storms

HE DID NOT KNOW where he was. His temples throbbed as though pounded by a hammer. As he fumbled in the cold semi-darkness that surrounded him, he wondered why his movements were so ponderous. He held his hand before he face; it was encased in a thick white glove. When he moved the hand to touch his aching head, he found it blocked by a clear, globular barrier.

I'm wearing a pressure suit.

Details trickled back. A cramped spherical space surrounded him, crammed with switches and dials. He knew this space well, having spent the better part of a year learning every square centimeter.

I'm in the LK Lander. Good. Now where am I?

All the gauges and indicators were dark. The only light was a pure white glow filtering in from a round porthole before him. Aleksey leaned towards it, but some force restrained him. In a reflexive motion honed by countless egress drills, his hands flew to his shoulders and unclasped his harness. He drifted forward, his motion strangely smooth and effortless. As the view through the porthole greeted him, his pain-clouded mind wondered: why had someone pinned a photograph to the window? The gently rolling hills outside were pure white, the sky black as ink.

The fog lifted. The realization struck like a thunderbolt.

I'm on the moon.

Everything came flooding back. The fiery liftoff of the N-1 rocket. The grueling three-day journey to the moon, packed like sardines in a Soyuz capsule that threatened to fail at every turn. The final handshake with Oleg, and the harrowing spacewalk from the Soyuz to the LK. As it had on his pioneering Voshkod II spacewalk, Aleksey's spacesuit had swelled in the vacuum. Bleeding pressure from the suit, he had risked the Bends as he struggled to squeeze through the LK's hatch. He remembered the tense descent, the silent but powerful kick of the Blok D rocket stage that sent him hurtling towards the moon. His landing radar had failed, leaving him blind. Using his knowledge of crater sizes, he had struggled to gauge his altitude and rate of descent. The vast bowl of the crater Copernicus had sprawled out beneath him, and he saw the tiny, insect-like shadow of the LK flitting among the boulders and rilles. Then…

Then what? Aleksey had blacked out. But why? What had happened? Aleksey reached to the circuit breaker panel by his knee. All the breakers had tripped, their red indicators gaping like banks of tiny mouths frozen in silent screams. Aleksey reset them. As the cabin lights and dials flickered to life, he snapped his eyes to the pressure gauge. The hull was intact; pressure was holding. Aleksey unlocked his neck ring and swung open his helmet visor, sighing with relief as cool cabin air flowed into the stifling confines of his suit. He then launched into his status checklist. The procedure had been etched into his mind through endless drills, and he performed it efficiently despite the disorienting fog of his pounding headache. Mercifully everything seemed in working order, though his radar remained inoperable. Strangely, the radio readouts wandered back and forth, the high-gain antennae scanning in vain for a signal. When Aleksey activated his radio headset, he winced as harsh static blared in his ear.

"Vostok, this is Mirny," he signaled. "Do you read me? This is Mirny. Over."

Nothing. He heard no reply among the crackling static. His hand flew over the radio control panel, trying every corrective action he was trained to apply. He found no signal.

What is going on? Aleksey pressed his face to the porthole, straining to the limits of his vision. But instead of the antenna on its short boom, he saw only black sky. Turning to the left, he saw nothing but lunar dust. A chill ran down his spine.

I'm sideways.

In his confusion and the moon's low gravity, he had not noticed the tilt. But now, he saw the horizon leaning askew outside the window. Something was very wrong.

Aleksey withdrew from the porthole. He did not panic. A cosmonaut never panicked; panic consumed precious time and oxygen. Instead, he took a deep breath and cooly took stock of the situation. He knew his craft leaned severely to one side, and that at least one radio antenna was damaged. But he knew not the extent of the damage, nor what had caused it. His plan of action was clear: reestablish communication with Oleg in the Soyuz, and correct the tilt so he could take off again. But he could accomplish neither from inside the cabin. He would have go outside.

Aleksey let his training take over. Consulting the booklet strapped to his wrist, he ran through his EVA checklist. He closed his suit, checked his seals and oxygen supply, and disconnected from the LK. When at last he was ready, he depressurized the cabin. He listened as the hum of the LK's systems faded to silence, leaving only the hiss of oxygen in his suit.

Here I go.

Aleksey grabbed the hatch release and pulled. It was stuck. Bracing against his seat, Aleksey placed his full weight upon the handle. At last it unlatched and the portal silently swung open. Aleksey did not peer out into the vista beyond; he had already begun turning round to back out through the hatch. He cursed as his elbows clanged against the equipment packing the tiny cabin. The LK had not been designed for comfort; indeed, throughout the craft's development the cosmonaut had almost seemed an afterthought, another component to be bolted into place among the nozzles and antennae. Aleksey had once heard an engineer ask a visiting official:

'Why risk the lives of our cosmonauts? We can learn just as much from our Lunokhod robots'.

'Because', snapped the official. 'A robot cannot represent the Soviet people'.

But you can, thought Aleksey. Just get back to earth.

Aleksey backed out through the hatch, twisting and shimmying as his bulky life-support backpack caught on the edges. His foot reached down to ladder's first rung, but found no purchase. His legs dangled in midair. Knowing the drop to be short, Aleksey released his grip and slowly drifted to a smooth touchdown. It was a peculiar feeling, like sinking to the bottom of a swimming pool. Safely on the ground, he lifted his foot and marveled at the crisp print his boot had left in the dust. Then he saw the tangled mess of bent tubing at his feet.

Aleksey jumped back in shock, nearly tripping over his own feet. His spacesuit was stiff and bulky; he felt like a child swaddled in thick winter clothes. He managed to stumble several paces back, and gaze upon his spacecraft.

The LK's spherical silver cabin leaned precariously to one side, its spindly legs crumpled beneath it like a spider crushed underfoot. One radio antenna lay crushed beneath this tangle; the other, ripped from its boom, dangled limply from its wire. Aleksey turned slowly around, surveying his surroundings. The LK lay in the midst of an empty plain of gently rolling white hills. Off in the distance, a line of sheer stone walls marked the rim of Copernicus. Amid such stark beauty, Aleksey's landing site looked strangely vulgar, like an otherworldly junkyard. To the north, the remains of a landing leg lay at the foot of the boulder which had severed it. To the east, the silver cylinder of the Blok D rocket stage rested like a discarded can of beets on a nearby rille. And to the south, the carcass of the wheeled Lunokhod robot, whose beacon should have guided Aleksey to a landing, stood dormant at the end of its winding path through the dust.

Aleksey approached the LK and inspected the severed antenna. The wire seemed intact. Holding the antenna above his head, he gazed up and searched for the Soyuz he knew was orbiting somewhere overhead. He suddenly froze as he beheld an incredible sight.

The moon shone brightly overhead. No: it was not the moon; he was on the moon. It was the earth, suspended like a blown glass marble in the black sky. Only then did it dawn on Aleksey just where he now stood. At this moment, he was the loneliest man in existence, farther from home than any man in history. The first man to set foot on another world. Aleksey shook his head in disbelief. He had once taken a train from Moscow to Vladivostok. How incomprehensibly huge that journey had been; how unfathomably vast seemed the earth. But it was a mere stone's throw next to the vast gulf he now stared across.

Aleksey's reverie did not last, for at last he spotted a faint point of light sailing across the black sky: the Soyuz. Or perhaps, he thought grimly, it was the Americans, who had launched one day after he and Oleg. Whatever the case, Aleksey would be glad to speak to another human being. He held the antenna like a torch, following the dim shooting star as it flew silently overhead. The antenna's servomotors panned and tilted the tiny dish, homing in on the Soyuz.

"Vostok, this is Mirny," he signaled. "Do you read me? This is Mirny. Over."

No reply. Static hissed in his headset.

"Vostok, Vostok, come in." said Aleksey, adjusting his aim. "This is Mirny. Come in."

Suddenly a faint, garbled voice could be heard, growing steadily clearer.

—…ny, thi…stok…peat, this is…stok. Aleksey, what happened? What is your status?

"Oleg!" said Aleksey joyously. "I'm fine. A small bump on the head, but fine."

—Good to hear. You had us worried there for a while.

"Guess I'm down to eight lives now."

—Six at last count. What is your status?

Aleksey paused, glancing to the tangled wreckage. "Critical," he said. "LPU severely damaged on landing. One leg has collapsed."

—Is your ascent stage intact?

"Yes, it looks like it," said Aleksey.

A pause.

—Mission control is consulting the engineers. Will advise.

"Roger that,"

Aleksey wedged the antenna into a bracket on the LK, freeing his hands. He then attempted to circle the craft, inspecting the damage from every angle. It was surprisingly slow going; he could neither run nor walk in the stiff suit and low gravity. With some brief experimentation, he learned to hop about with both feet together, like some lunar kangaroo. He laughed like a child as he bounded along, clearing great distances with each bound. He had flown the fastest jets past the speed of sound, but nothing compared to this. This was flying.

But reality soon came crashing down as the radio crackled again..

—Aleksey, what is the angle of the LK? said Oleg.

"I would say…about fifty degrees from the vertical."

There was a long pause, marked only by the occasional crackle in Aleksey's earpiece.

"Oleg?" called Aleksey. "Oleg? What do they say?"

Still nothing.

"Oleg…"

Aleksey noticed something strange: his heartbeat, pounding rapidly in his ears.

—No go, Oleg finally said,—The engineers say the angle is too steep for liftoff. The gyros can't handle it.

"Alright…" said Aleksey, turning to face the LK. "I'll override the automatic system, then. Take off manually…"

—Negative. The engineers say it won't work. The thrusters aren't strong enough to right you at that angle.

"Goddamn it, Oleg!" Aleksey snapped. "You ask those damned slide-rule jockeys what the hell I can do!"

Silence.

—…will advise.

Aleksey took a deep breath, fighting the pulse that pounded in his head. Yet try as he might, he could not stop the creeping specter of dread. If the engineers were right, any attempt to take off would turn him into a ballistic missile, arcing high over the surface before slamming back into the ground. He could not risk it—not in the LK's current condition. What, then? Aleksey's eyes frantically scanned the crushed lander, scouring every square inch. His gaze finally landed on the intact landing strut, jutting from the LK like a swimmer's foot testing the waters. Something clicked.

What if…

"Oleg," he said with urgency, bounding towards the LK. "Tell mission control I'm removing the landing leg. That should right the ascent stage."

—Say again? asked Oleg.

"I'm removing the landing leg," Aleksey repeated. "Whether the eggheads like it or not."

—…roger that.

Aleksey opened the utility compartment at the base of the LK, which held the tools and scientific instruments he was to have deployed on the surface: seismographs and cosmic ray detectors, rakes and shovels, and the Soviet flag with its collapsible pole. Tucked in the corner was a pitifully small canvas tool bag, which Aleksey clipped to his suit before clumsily clambering up the landing leg. It was then that he realized the absurdity of his situation. He had always imagined his first steps on the moon as a hallowed, momentous event. He would slowly step down the ladder, pausing before the last rung. He would deliver the speech the Moscow writers had prepared for him, and slowly drop down to the lunar soil. There he would plant the flag and stand at attention, saluting this glorious achievement of the Soviet Union and its people. But he felt no more glorious than a farmer, repairing his tractor by the side of a dusty road.

"I'm at the leg," he announced. "It will take less than an hour; there are only five…"

Aleksey broke off, staring at the leg in shock. He had studied the LK in almost microscopic detail, learning every nut and bolt. He had read every design revision, and inspected every LK in person. Yet instead of the five bolts he knew secured the leg, he saw before him a neat weld.

—Aleksey, what was that? Say again, please?

"Uh…Oleg?" said Aleksey. "Did they change the LK design before we launched?"

—Not that I know of. Why?

Aleksey rummaged through the tool bag, searching for a saw or cutters. He found none.

"Detaching landing leg not possible…they welded it."

—I will ask mission control. Do you have another idea?

Aleksey did not. His mind was a blank. For the first time, he felt his hands trembling. There was no way out—none that he could see. The ground was falling away under his feet. He cursed at this the seemingly insubstantial obstacle before him. It had probably taken a factory worker two seconds to lay down, but it was more secure a barrier than the thickest prison door. Alexei had travelled a quarter-million kilometers across the gulf of space; now his return was blocked by five centimeters of weld. At once, the truth he had held at bay for so long came crashing back: he would die here. He would never see the earth; the blue sky and the trees. His lifeless body, preserved by the cold and vacuum, would stare for all eternity at a black sky, without even a proper grave. For a brief moment a thought flashed in his mind: perhaps he would dig his own grave, before the end came. It was such a strange thought: digging his own grave in the lunar soil…

The lunar soil…

No!

Suddenly, Aleksey scrambled off the LK, gently touching down on the ground.

You will not die here.

"Oleg!" he called into his headset. "I'm going to dig. Under the leg. That should work: it should right the ascent stage."

—…roger that. Going around the far side now; will reestablish contact in one half-hour.

"Understood," said Aleksey. Then the radio went dead.

Aleksey returned to the utility compartment and snapped together a collapsible sample shovel. Then, kneeling by the landing leg's saucer-like footpad, he dug. It was painfully slow work, the stiff joints of his suit restricting his movement. He soon felt the strain in his muscles; his helmet fogged with moisture. During Voskhod II, it had taken such effort to reenter the spacecraft that his boots had filled to the knees with sweat. But he had no choice but to fight on, for failure would have stranded him in orbit. This in mind, Aleksey kept digging shovelful by pathetic shovelful. He marveled at the dust's otherworldly behavior. Without air, the dust did not billow; it flew in perfectly straight lines, plummeting to the ground like handfuls of lead shot.

Aleksey was finally rewarded as the landing leg lurched, falling a few centimeters into the shallow crater he had dug beneath it. It is working, he thought with a faint smile.

Resting for a few moments, Aleksey glanced at his watch. His heart dropped. He had been digging for a half hour. He did a quick mental sum; at this rate, it would take him 12 hours to level the craft. Flipping open the control panel on his chest, he checked his oxygen supply:

Six hours.

The suit held oxygen ten hours, but his exertions had consumed oxygen at a furious rate. The LK held a further 12 hours. Even if all went well, it would be a close race.

—Aleksey,—Are you still there? What is your progress?

"Slow," Aleksey panted. "But I think it will work."

—How long?

"Ten hours. Maybe," said Aleksey grimly. "I have oxygen for sixteen."

A pause.

—Can you do it in five?

Even through the crackling static, Aleksey could hear fear in Oleg's voice.

"Oleg, what's going on?"

No answer.

"Oleg! Tell me what's going on! Is there something wrong with Vostok?"

—Vostok is fine. Can you do it in five hours, yes or no?

"No," said Aleksey. "I need at least ten. Why are…"

Suddenly, another, deeper voice came on the radio.

—Comrade Leonov, said the voice.

—On behalf of a grateful nation, I would like to personally thank you for your valiant service to the State.

Aleksey gaped, incredulous: it was Premier Brezhnev.

—The Soviet Union and its people are proud of you. You will always be remembered.

"No! I will return, Comrade Premier! I just need…"

But Brezhnev was gone. Oleg's voice crackled back onto the radio.

—I'm sorry, Aleksey, I have my orders.

"Wait!" Aleksey screamed. "Oleg! Why!? Why are you doing this? I can fix this! I just need time! Tell them! Tell them I just need time!"

—I will tell Svetlana.

"Oleg? Oleg! Oleg, come back!" Aleksey's mind reeled. The bastards! he thought. Why? Why had they marooned him? The Soyuz was intact; Oleg had plenty of oxygen. So why…

There could be only one explanation: the Americans.

It made perfect sense; their Saturn V was more powerful than the N-1. They had closed the gap. Aleksey thought back to his pre-flight briefing, and the Moscow man who told him: 'If this does not succeed, and the Americans beat us, remember: this mission never existed. We were not beaten to the moon; we were never competing.'

I will tell Svetlana you died a hero. Aleksey knew what this meant. At this very moment, an official Moscow was banging away at his typewriter, composing Aleksey's obituary. Just a few years ago he would have toiled in a darkroom, expunging Aleksey's image from every photo of the cosmonaut corps. All mention of his name would vanish from print. Aleksey would cease to be. But he was too famous now; his disappearance would not go unnoticed. How would they explain his death, he wondered? A plane crash, most likely, just like Gagarin. They would swear Oleg to secrecy, and claim the N-1 launch was unmanned. And as Aleksey lay dead on this barren plain, the Americans would win a race that had never been. It was that simple.

"No!" cried Aleksey, assaulting the ground with renewed fury. Oleg needed another orbit before he could fire his engines; Aleksey had an hour. Moon dust flew all about as he manically dug, coating his white spacesuit in a dark grey blanket. Aleksey's arms burned under the strain. Yet centimeter by desperate centimeter, the landing leg lowered into the pit.

Yes, that's it. Keep digging, Aleksey. Keep digging. You can do it.

Suddenly, the shovel struck something solid; but for the vacuum, it would have made a sharp clang. Aleksey thrust again; the shovel was again halted. Heart racing, he fell to his stomach and clawed frantically at the pit with his gloved fingers. Uncovering a small patch of pale grey stone, he dug outwards to find its edge. He did not find it. The stone extended far beyond the pit, too large to dig around and too heavy to move. It was over.

In defeat and exhaustion, Aleksey collapsed and rolling onto his back. Gazing up into the empty sky, he saw the tiny fleck of the Soyuz emerge from behind the horizon. The star twinkled brightly as the engines ignited, wrenching it free from the moon's grasp. Like a meteor it crossed the sky and sailed silently into the darkness. Then it was gone.

Lying in the dust, gasping with exhaustion, Aleksey suddenly thought of Vladimir Komarov. He remembered the night before the ill-fated flight of Soyuz 1, standing on the gantry with Vladimir and Yuri Gagarin. The floodlit rocket towered over them like a cenotaph. Vladimir was ashen-faced, hand trembling as he raised his last cigarette to his lips.

'You know,' Vladimir had said, smiling grimly. 'The engineers found 203 faults. They told this to the politicians. You know what they said? "It is Lenin's birthday. Nothing can go wrong".'

'Vladimir,' Gagarin had pleaded. 'Why are you doing this?'

'Because, Yuri,' said Vladimir, tears welling in his eyes. 'If I don't, they'd send you.'

Aleksey could still hear Vladimir's final transmission ringing in his ears, the blood-curdling scream as the crippled spacecraft hurtled back through the atmosphere. With his last breaths Vladimir had sent his wife his love, then cursed the engineers and mission planners who had betrayed him. There was little left now at the impact site but a crater and a few scraps of aluminum. They had placed what remained of Vladimir in an open casket, the blackened chunks like overdone steaks laid grotesquely on the white silk pillows. Throughout the surreal, vulgar affair they had made great speeches, declaring Vladimir Komarov a great hero. A postage stamp with his smiling face had appeared the next week. For Aleksey, there would be nothing to display.

Aleksey lay on his back for a long time, staring blankly into the darkness. He was only roused when a shrill siren blared in his ear. With great effort, he reached to his chest display and read his oxygen supply: five minutes. He should have lain still, allowing anoxia to carry him off to a peaceful end. But he did not. Some spark—some notion—compelled him to lift himself out of the dust. Stumbling back to the LK, he slumped in the open hatch and connected his suit to the lander's oxygen supply. As he lay there, he reached below the seat and activated the magnetic recorder. When at last his suit was replenished, Aleksey dropped to the ground and surveyed his domain. He was truly alone on this alien world, like The Little Prince on his asteroid.

"To anyone who finds this," he narrated into the recorder. "I am speaking from the Ocean of Storms on the 19th of July, 1969. I have crash landed here, three kilometers from the crater Copernicus. It is very beautiful here. It is almost like the Ukrainian steppe after a heavy snowfall. The boulders are like hay bales when they are buried in snow…or the big balls of snow children like to roll. The sky is very black; I can see very few stars. just the earth and the sun."

Aleksey knelt and scooped up a handful of lunar dust, letting it sift through his fingers.

"Everything looks white in the sunlight, like snow. But the dust is grey, like…gunpowder. It sticks together, almost like it is wet. It gets all over everything; my suit is covered…"

Aleksey continued to narrate as he pulled the scientific instruments from the utility compartment. One by one he carried these devices to the perimeter of the landing site, assembling them according to his wrist checklist. He doubted anyone would ever find these instruments, or whether the data would be intact if they did. It did not matter; this was all he could do. Finally, only one item remained in the compartment: the flag. Aleksey reached for it, then stopped. His fingers trembled mere centimeters from the tightly-rolled band of cloth.

Aleksey took a deep breath, then dropped his hand. Brandishing a shovel, he turned away.

"I have taken a sample of every kind of rock I could find," he said some hours later, sealing a pebble into a hermetic sample canister. "I hope it is a fairly representative collection. I have put them under the seat of the LK. If they are still alive when you find this, please give some to Viktoria and Oskana, as a gift from their father. Svetlana and my two beautiful daughters, if you are listening to this, I want you to know that I love you and I did everything to come back to you. I am looking at the earth now. I wish you could be here to see it; it is like a drop of dew that you can see the world through, or…a ball of blown glass. No, it is beyond words. Oh, how I wish I had my paints or my sketchbook here. Viktoria, do you remember when you said God must have been a painter? I think you were right. I am looking at the earth, wishing I could see you. Look up to the moon, my darlings, and know that I am always thinking of you."

As if to end his epitaph, the shrill siren rang like a knell in his ear. Aleksey did not return to the LK. Relaxing his legs, he drifted gently down until he knelt in the lunar dust. Each breath grew ever more labored; he felt faint and dizzy. He reached into a pocket and removed a handful of mementos he was to have left on the surface: postal covers, a small flag signed by Premier Brezhnev, and metal tokens bearing the red star, hammer and sickle. Hidden among these he had smuggled a personal token, wrapped in airtight cellophane: a photograph of Aleksey, Svetlana and their daughters, smiling on the front steps of their dacha. Pocketing the other tokens, Aleksey placed the photo in the dust before him. It had been a risk smuggling it here; had the Politburo found out, they would have expelled him from the cosmonaut ranks. But this no longer mattered. Strength ebbing, he raised his gaze to the brilliant blue orb glowing overhead. With his last conscious breath, he spoke into the microphone.

"My name is Aleksey Arkhipovich Leonov. I came for mankind."

... ...

Above the planet on a wing and a prayer. My grubby halo, a vapor trail in the empty air. Above the clouds I see my shadow fly. Out of the corner of my wandering eye. A dream unthreatened by the morning light. Could blow this soul right through the roof of the night

—David Gilmour, 'Learning to Fly'

Saturn V replica, rocket park at Marshall Spaceflight Centre, Huntsville Alabama, USA.
Photo by Gilles Messier, April 2010.

The Sky is Calling

WE STOPPED IN AN anonymous field, no different from countless others that had rolled past along the dusty roads. A patch of yellow scrub dotted with dark clumps of trees, meandering snake fences and whitewashed farmhouses—Anywhere, rural USA. Here our weary journey ground to a halt, at least for the moment. As the car came to rest, Saliya slumped back in the driver's seat and was at once asleep. Beside him, Raakesh too was soon snoring away. Spoiled by years of comfortable beds, neither I nor Javier could find rest in the back seat. I staggered out into the field and collapsed in the long grass, where I lay still, gazing at a clear Alabama sky.

I closed my bleary eyes and listened to the cicadas buzzing. What were we doing here, so far from home? This field lay at the end of a four-month odyssey, a symphony of looming disaster that, in the last two days, had reached its violent, spectacular crescendo. And for what, I thought? The whole mad drama—through which I had lost sleep, grades, blood, sanity, and very nearly my life—had revolved around the unlikeliest of objects: a Lunar Rover, an ungainly assembly of aluminum tubes, chains and bicycle wheels. We had come to Huntsville to compete, to pit our Rover against the best Universities in the world. In the shadow of towering rockets that had once hurtled men into space, we would turn our months of careful design and construction into pure metal motion, taking our rightful place among the builders of tomorrow. Such were our ambitions. Instead, we entered a living nightmare.

It all began in with our project leader's abrupt resignation in January. And there it should have ended. But we were cocksure young engineers; we could solve any problem, meet any deadline. For our brashness, we received nothing but grief: countless hours hunched over machine tools, feverishly shaping metal until our hands were raw and burnt. As though possessed by a demon, the Rover fought us at every turn; every nut, bolt and screw an exercise in frustration. Many a long sleepless night was spent in the shop, desperately wrestling the unruly mechanism into submission. The thirsty metal soaked up our blood and sweat, yielding by inches, but when the deadline arrived we had little to show for our labours: the rover could not roll one foot. If it was foolish to proceed before, it was doubly so now. But fools we were. Against all logic, we loaded our useless contraption into a van and set off on the long drive south.

Two days later, as we pulled up beneath the futuristic buildings of the Marshall Spaceflight Centre, our spirits were high. The repairs, we thought, would be a mere matter of hours: a handful of sprockets to align, chains to tension, and brakes to install. In no time our riders, pedaling with all their might, would send our creation trundling to victory down the gravel track that snaked through the rocket garden. But the Demon had followed us south. Hours became two desperate days under the baking Alabama sun, wailing on the stubborn chassis with wrenches and hammers as part after part failed. During construction, we had held few design reviews; we had no time for such formalities. All fires were extinguished on the spot, design changes hastily drafted and rushed to the machine shop. Now, every poor decision that had crept into the design, unchecked and unchallenged in our haste, finally caught up with us. As other teams' streamlined contraptions sailed smoothly past between the gleaming Redstone and Saturn rockets, we squabbled like rabid dogs over the lifeless carcass of our rover. But the foolish persistence of the young is a powerful force, and when the final disqualification deadline at last crept up on us, every problem had been miraculously beaten into tenuous submission. Our rover, rickety as it was, could at last take the track. Our riders, who had waited impatiently on the sidelines for two days, mounted the machine and slowly pedaled off to their triumphant debut.

They had rolled barely one foot when with a loud pop, a wheel suddenly collapsed, the chassis lurching to one side. We rushed forward to investigate. The axle had snapped, having somehow been made of aluminum. It was one flaw among hundreds, riddling the Rover like malignant tumors. Our hearts sank: it was over. Despite our best efforts to bring this machine into the world, kicking and screaming, it had staggered mere inches before collapsing, dead. The Demon had won. There was nothing to do but gather its remains and return home; University exams awaited us up north. Along the way we would make a pilgrimage to the Air and Space Museum in Washington, taking solace in the technical achievements of others. Perhaps we could salvage something from this wretched mess.

But with the Rover dead, the Demon had found new hosts. As Javier and I left Huntsville in the fading evening light, the Rover's broken remains littering the back of the van, the Demon cruelly reminded us that while it took much to build a complex machine, it took little to destroy it. It was a single wrong turn that lead us down that dark, winding country road, and a single sharp corner that sent us careening into the ditch. In that instant of frozen time, as the sharp lines of trees burst from the darkness, I did not fear death. I only sighed that it should end here, in some Alabama backwoods, at the nadir of a career—a life—not yet begun. I had long seen myself dying an old man, behind me a lifetime of watching my creations sail off into the sky—or high above the earth, guiding a sleek machine into the unknown. But this thought was soon gone. In the last split second, I braced for the crushing impact. The world exploded in a churning maelstrom of screaming metal as a hail of nuts, bolts, wrenches and hammers—the ashes of our failed ambition—rained down all around us. Then, at once, all was dark and still. I heard my own breathing in the silence; I was still alive. When Javier and I crawled from the wreckage, we discovered, to our amazement, that we had not a single scratch or bruise upon us. The Demon, it seemed, had a sense of humor. It had spared us a swift end so we could endure a longer torment. The next day was spent in a frantic, confused haze as we scrambled to untangle this new mess. Amid the maddening negotiations for wrecking, insurance and rentals, we had to endure the bitterest blow of all: watching our Rover- four months of our lives- cut up for scrap. The last we had heard, its remains reinforced a potting shed—the most use it had ever seen. Through all of this, only the legendary Southern Hospitality of the locals helped soften the blows.

Now, twenty-four hours behind schedule, we raced a grueling marathon to the northern border and our looming examinations—the next milestone on our long journey to becoming engineers. What was the point, I thought? I had already sacrificed so much to this project, to the notion that the physical, working product of my two hands would prove my engineering prowess more than any mathematical scribbles on paper. I had postponed classes to work in the machine shop, neglected assignments to attend assembly sessions, and now I would miss my examinations. But still I had failed. Before leaving Huntsville, I had stood in the shadow of the mighty Saturn V, the rocket that had sent men to the moon. Fifty years before, armed with little more than slide rules, great men had made this towering metal skyscraper fly. I, on the other hand, could not make a glorified bicycle roll two feet.

Suddenly, a man-shaped shadow blocked the sun.

"Hey, are you okay, man?" said Javier, looming overhead.

"Yes," I said. "Just tired."

"You and me both," he said. "Hey, you want to set off those fireworks?"

"Sure, why not?" I sighed, stiffly rising from the grass. From the car trunk I pulled two bulging paper bags, our haul from two nights before. Defeated and dejected, we sought cathartic release in that irresistible confectionary: an American fireworks store. We had planned to take these spoils home, but the crash changed our minds. We did not wish to add smuggling charges to our misfortunes.

I placed an empty soda bottle on the ground as a makeshift launch pad, then began the mayhem with the larger rockets. These whistled into the sky and burst with sharp reports and showers of sparks, somewhat dulled against the sunlit sky. We fired roman candles like pistols, set off strings of ladyfingers, and demolished ant hills with M-80s, laughing like hyenas with childlike abandon. But something was missing. In the back of my mind a hunger smoldered, an itch that no sharp report, shower of sparks, or Technicolor flame could scratch. This thirst went unsated as I dug through the bag for ever-more spectacular incendiaries. But as my hand emerged with a cluster of bottle rockets, the truth dawned on me. Silently I snapped off the long red tails and jammed each rocket one atop the other, forming a tall stack.

"What are you doing?" asked Javier.

"Staging," I explained. Just as real rockets had multiple engines and stages, so would mine. As each rocket burst at the apex of its flight, it would light the fuse on the next. This humble firework would become a proper missile, worthy of the engineers launching her.

Javier looked skeptical as I held up my completed creation. Ignoring him, I scuttled through the grass in search of an insect Gagarin to make the first flight into the unknown. As no volunteers were forthcoming—they being perhaps as wary as Javier of their craft's integrity—an inert payload of smoke bombs was substituted. The rickety, disjointed stack, leaning atop its glass-bottle launch pad, was no majestic Saturn V. If it flew apart, scattering pinwheeling trails of fire across the sky, it would be par for the course on this miserable voyage. I had nothing to lose. Without ceremony, I knelt down and lit the fuse. As it sputtered and hissed, I hastily stepped back; despairing as I was, I had no desire to receive a flaming rocket to the face.

Several tense seconds later, with a whistling hiss and burst of white smoke, the rocket sprang from the bottle. It all happened so quickly; I hadn't even time to register the quick, rhythmic whoosh-bang-whoosh-bang. It wasn't until the smoke bombs burst in a great dome above me, trailing coloured streamers to the ground, that I realized: it had worked. Immediately I found myself transported to a field much like this one, not one year ago. I lay behind an earthen berm, gripping a small yellow control box. A wire snaked from the box over the berm, down to a strange contraption lying in the gully: a black cylinder strapped to a concrete block, festooned in a confusing tangle of silver pipes and tubes. I swallowed hard as I placed my finger on the firing button. The month before had been an endless procession of disappointments: I had seen that jury-rigged pile of plumbing hiss, smoke, sputter, and explode—but despite my best efforts I could coax no life from it. Still I had returned to try again; there was nothing else to do. With a final sigh, I braced for another inevitable failure.

"5, 4, 3, 2, 1…fire in the hole!"

I hit the switch.

My eyes widened in disbelief, my jaw hanging agape. The sound that emerged from behind the berm was not the dry hiss I had long become accustomed to, but a deafening roar. I stuck my head above the berm, then immediately withdrew it as the piercing shriek stabbed my eardrums. In that split second, I had seen all I needed: a bright, hot jet shooting from the mouth of the cylinder, its stream broken into neat glowing diamonds of flame. I let out a loud whoop: my rocket engine worked. With this unlikely contraption, cobbled together from hardware-store parts, I had harnessed the forces of nature. At that moment, as that roar thundered across the empty field, my road to the stars opened before me….

I stood still for many long minutes, staring at the sky, before at last I dropped my gaze. When my eyes met Javier's, a broad grin broke across my face. I immediately dropped to my knees, hastily assembling a new missile. In science and engineering, after all, results had to be repeatable; that first success might have been a fluke. As I knelt by the bottle with a cigarette lighter, I was no longer here, in this time and place. This empty field was a Cosmodrome. The rocket loomed majestically on its pad, boldly lit by crisscrossing beams of floodlights. I stood at a console, finger on the launch button, status updates crackling through my headphones. One by one the launch controllers raised their thumbs; we were go for launch. Out on the pad, the gantry arms swung gracefully away, leaving the rocket standing alone, liquid oxygen fog streaming impatiently down its sides. Eyes fixed upon the clock on the wall, I called out the countdown.

"Ten, nine, eight, … two, one… Ignition!"

There was no earth-shaking roar, no roiling cloud of smoke or geyser of flame as the rocket gracefully lifted from the pad; only that sharp whoosh, and the spreading starburst canopy of coloured smoke signaling that, once again, the makeshift contraption had worked. Though it had only risen ten feet, my bottle rocket stack differed from an orbital launcher by a mere matter of degrees. The principles were the same; only the scale differed. The fact still remained: armed with nothing but knowledge and intuition, I had created something more, something new. Such was the essence of an engineer, beyond all the math and steam tables: the intuitive ability to build, to create, something no textbook could teach. I was already an engineer; the rest was mere formality. Some day, somehow, I would wade through all the lectures and examinations and answer my true calling. And what of the occasional failure? How many sleek missiles had those great rocket men watched burst into flames before the first of their creations lifted gracefully into the wild blue yonder? The Rover had failed, but this rocket had succeeded. It was as simple as that. As the last wisps of smoke faded into the azure sky, I glanced at Javier and smiled.

"Let's push on," I said.

Soyuz TMA-18 capsule on the ground, Kazakhstan, September 25, 2010 [Bill Ingalls Photo]
engadget.com/photos/soyuz-tma-18-space-capsule-landing/#3438590

Physicist Luis Alvarez in his laboratory, 1940s
corbisimages.com/stock-photo/rights-managed/BE064733/luis-alvarez-in-his-laboratory-with-a

Historical and Technical Notes

The stories in this collection are extensively researched and grounded in fact. This section is provided for the benefit of readers curious as to the historical basis of these works.

The Girl at Panel 857

This story was inspired by the Manhattan Project, the Allied effort to develop the atomic bomb. Overseen by U.S. Army Major Leslie Groves and civilian physicist J. Robert Oppenheimer, the Manhattan Project was a monumental industrial undertaking, comparable in scale and cost ($28 billion in today's dollars) to the Apollo program that landed men on the moon.

In addition to developing designs for atomic bombs, Manhattan Project scientists had to produce sufficient quantities of the elements Uranium and Plutonium to build the bombs themselves. Feasible weapon designs were quickly narrowed down to two: gun-type and implosion-type.

In a gun-type weapon, an explosive charge propels a mass of fissile material down a gun barrel into another, forming a supercritical mass that undergoes nuclear detonation. Though this design was simple, it had one major flaw: the need for Uranium-235. The U-235 isotope is the only fissile element found in nature, but comprises only 0.72% of all natural Uranium (the rest consisting of non-fissile U-238). This meant that thousands of tons of uranium had to be refined to produce the 34 pounds of 90% enriched U-235 the bomb required. Manhattan Project scientists developed three enrichment methods to separate U-235 from U-238, which were simultaneously employed at the Oak Ridge National Laboratory in Tennessee. The first method, Gaseous Diffusion, passed Uranium Hexafluoride gas through a series of Teflon membranes. As the lighter U-235 diffused faster than U-238, at each stage the gas became increasingly enriched in U-235. The second method, Thermal Diffusion, exploited the fact that lighter U-235 would diffuse preferentially towards the top of a heated fluid column. The third method, the Calutron (named after the University of California), was an enormous mass spectrometer. Uranium was vaporized and the resulting ionized gas accelerated past a powerful magnetic field. U-235 and U-238, having different masses, followed different curved paths and were collected in different compartments. For maximum efficiency, the ion beam had to be constantly refocused, a task originally assigned to technicians. When the technicians were needed for other projects, female high school graduates were hired to operate the control panels. The Calutron Girls worked in complete ignorance of the true nature of their work, which most did not discover until nearly 50 years later. The character of Vera Mason is modelled on the real-life Gladys Owens, who appears in the right foreground in the photograph accompanying the story.

The gun-type weapon, code-named Little Boy, was dropped on Hiroshima on August 6, 1945. It was never tested prior to deployment, as only enough U-235 for one bomb had been produced. Furthermore, the scientists believed the design to be almost guaranteed to work. The implosion-type bomb, however, was another matter. In this design, a set of high-explosive 'lenses' compress a spherical core of fissile material to criticality. This bomb has the advantage of using Plutonium-239, a synthetic element that can be bred in large quantities using nuclear reactors. But the explosive lens system was considered insufficiently proven to warrant testing. Thus, on July 16, 1945, the world's first nuclear bomb (code-named Trinity and nicknamed The Gadget) was detonated near Alamogordo, New Mexico, with a yield of 20 kilotons of TNT. On August 9, a weaponized version of The Gadget—code-named Fat Man—was dropped on Nagasaki. Six days later, Japan surrendered and WWII ended. Today, almost all nuclear weapons are implosion-type due to the relative ease of producing Pu-239.

Hypothermia

Dr. Sigmund Rascher (1909-1945) of the Luftwaffe and SS conducted numerous experiments on human subjects at the Dachau Concentration Camp from 1941-1944. In addition to determining the effects of freezing on the human body, Rascher investigated methods for safely rewarming a hypothermic patient. Rapid rewarming in hot baths was found to be the best method, though this technique can sometimes induce 'rewarming shock'—a rapid drop in blood pressure caused by circulation suddenly returning to limbs. At the time, many people believed that body heat was the best rewarming method and that such 'animal warmth' somehow acted differently from artificial heat. To test this, Rascher forced Gypsy women from the Ravensbruck Concentration Camp to have sex with frozen test subjects. He found this method to be largely ineffective.

In addition to his hypothermia research, Rascher investigated the physiological effects of high-altitude flight, subjecting Dachau prisoners to rapid decompression in a hypobaric chamber. Another experiment sought to determine how long humans could survive drinking only seawater. Subjects became so dehydrated that they would lick freshly-mopped floors. Rascher and his wife Nini also championed a theory that population growth could be accelerated by raising the maximum child-bearing age. The fact that Rascher's wife had born three children after the age of 48 was used in Nazi propaganda to promote this idea. When it was discovered that all four children had actually been bought or kidnapped, the Raschers were arrested and executed at Dachau in 1945.

In contrast to Dr. Josef Mengele at Auschwitz, Rascher carried out his experiments with extreme scientific rigor. The results of his freezing experiments remain the only accurate data available on hypothermia in humans. As a result, there has been considerable controversy over whether Rascher's data can ethically be used.

Képi Blanc

The French Foreign Legion was established by King Louis Phillipe in 1831 to allow failed revolutionaries, criminals, foreign nationals and other disruptive elements to fight for France. Deployed in defence of French colonies such as Algeria and Indochina, the Legion quickly developed a fearsome reputation—immortalized by their unofficial motto Marche ou Crève (March or Die). Their legend was cemented at the 1863 Battle of Camaron in Mexico, when 65 Legionnaires fought nearly to the last man against 2,000 Mexican soldiers. The last six Legionnaires charged the enemy with bayonets; the three that survived were allowed to return home by the stunned Mexicans.

The Legion is most commonly associated with Morocco, where, from 1892 to 1926, it defended French colonists against local tribes. During this period, the Legion acquired a romantic mystique, famously captured in P.C. Wren's classic 1924 novel Beau Geste. The Legion became popular with criminals and other down-on-their-luck men seeking a fresh start; today, however, Legion recruitment is more selective.

During WWII, the Legion fought the pivotal yet largely forgotten Battle of Bir Hakeim. From May 26 to June 11, 1942, 4,000 Legionnaires defended the small Libyan fort against three German and Italian tank divisions commanded by General Erwin Rommel. Though the French were forced to retreat, they had bought the British forces time to regroup. The German advance across North Africa was halted at the First Battle of El Alamein one month later. In the words of French General Bernard Saint-Hillier, A grain of sand had curbed the Axis advance, which reached Al-Alamein only after the arrival of the rested British divisions: this grain of sand was Bir Hakeim.

After the war, the Legion was again deployed to defend France's crumbling empire. During the First Indochina War (1946-1954) it suffered catastrophic losses against the Viet Minh, with several battalions being effectively wiped out. During the 1954 Battle of Dien Bien Phu, the 2nd Foreign Parachute Division, attempting to reinforce the besieged French fort, jumped at suicidally low altitudes to avoid anti-aircraft fire. The fort was overrun, however, and France lost control of Indochina.

The Legion was next deployed during the Algerian War of Independence (1954-62), where it fought a brutal counter-insurgency against Front de Liberation Nationale (FLN) rebels. When French President Charles de Gaulle granted Algeria its independence in 1961, disgruntled factions within the French army attempted to overthrow him. The coup quickly collapsed, however, and the 1st Foreign Parachute Regiment (REP) was disbanded for its role in the putsch.

The Foreign Legion continues to fight in defence of France's foreign interests in countries such as the Democratic Republic of Congo, Côte D'ivoire, Kosovo and Afghanistan. On parade, the Legionnaires maintain their distinctive iconography: the Képi blanc (a white, cylindrical-crowned cap) and the flaming grenade emblem.

In this story I have made extensive use of soldiers' songs (see the list of first verses at the end of this note). Panzerlied remains the official song of the German armoured corps.

The tune, with different lyrics, is also sung by the Foreign Legion as Képi Blanc. The Legion's official marching song, Le Boudin, translates as Blood Sausage, referencing the red bedroll carried by Pre-WWI Legionnaires. The song refers to the fact that King Leopold of Belgium forbade his subjects from joining the Legion.

Many civilian songs have become popular among soldiers throughout history. During WWII, Radio Belgrade regularly broadcast Lale Andersen's rendition of Lili Marlene, a tender ballad about a soldier and his sweetheart. The song became an instant favorite among Axis and Allied troops, who both tuned in to the broadcasts. In 1961 famous French singer Edith Piaf dedicated her recording of Non, Je ne regrette rien to the Foreign Legion; when the 1st REP was disbanded following the Algiers Putsch, the Legionnaires emerged from their barracks singing the song.

... ...

First verses of soldiers' songs in "Képi Blac":

Panzerlied
(traditional song; lyrics by Kurt Wiehle, 1933;
official song of the German armoured corps)

Ob's stürmt oder schneit,
ob die sonne uns lacht
Der tag gluhend heiss,
oder eiskalt die nacht
Versaubt sind die gesichter,
doch froh ist under sinn
Ja unser sinn
Es braust unser panzer
im Sturmwind dahin

Whether it storms or snows,
whether the sun shines upon us
The day glowing hot,
or the ice cold of the night
Dusty are our faces,
but joyful are our minds
Yes, so are our minds
Our tanks roar forward
through the storm

Képi Blanc
(adapted from Panzerlied by the French Foreign Legion)

Puisqu'il nous faut vivre
et lutter dans la souffrance
Le jour est venu
où nous imposerons au front
La force de nos âmes,
la force de nos cœurs
et de nos bras
Foulant la boue sombre,
vont les Képis blancs

For we must live
and fight in suffering
The day has come
when they'll send us to the front
The strength of our souls,
the strength of our hearts
and of our arms
Ignoring the somber mud,
go the Képis blancs

Le Boudin
(c. 1860-1880; song of the French Foreign Legion)

Tiens, voilà du boudin,

Pour les Alsaciens, les Suisses
et les Lorrains
Pour les Belges y en a plus,
Ce sont des tireurs au cul

Here's some blood sausage,
For the Alsatians, Swiss
and Lorrains
For the Belgians there's none,
They're a bunch of lazy shirkers

Lili Marlene
(Poem by Hans Liep, 1915; music Norbert Schultze, 1938;
original recording by Lale Andersen, 1939; English lyrics Tommy Connor, 1944)

Vor der Kaserne,
Vor dem großen Tor,
Stand eine Laterne,
Und steht sie noch davor,
So woll'n wir uns da wieder seh'n,
Bei der Laterne wollen wir steh'n,
Wie einst,
Lili Marleen

Underneath the lantern
By the barrack gate,
Darling I remember
The way you used to wait.
T'was there that you whispered

tenderlythat you loved me;
You'd always be
My Lili of the lamplight,
My own Lili Marlene

Non, Je ne regrette rien
(music Charles Dumont, lyrics Michel Vaucaire, 1956;
recorded by Edith Piaf, 1960.)

Non, rien de rien
Non, je ne regrette rien
Ni le bien que on m'a fait
Ni le mal
Tout ça m'est bien égale
No, nothing at all

No, I regret nothing
Neither the good
that's been done for me
Nor the bad
It's all the same to me

… … …

The Fisherman and the Genie

This story was inspired by David Hahn, the so-called Radioactive Boy Scout, who, in 1994, at the age of 17, attempted to build a small nuclear reactor in his parents' potting shed in Commerce Township, Michigan. Hahn had been experimenting with radioactive elements for several years, extracting Americium from smoke detectors and Thorium from gas lantern mantles. His original intention was to obtain a sample of every element on the periodic table, a quest inspired by reading the 1950s-vintage Golden Book of Chemistry Experiments. Hahn, a Boy Scout, then decided to earn his Atomic Energy merit badge by building a small working model of a breeder reactor. His crude reactor was assembled from cubes of Thorium-laced ash wrapped in tinfoil. It was too small to attain critical mass, but it generated enough radiation to be measured down the block. Alarmed, Hahn tried to dismantle his reactor, but the police eventually discovered his handiwork. The potting shed and all of Hahn's equipment was extricated and placed in a nuclear waste repository. Hahn later dropped out of school and joined the Navy. In 1997, he was convicted of larceny for stealing Americium-containing smoke detectors from his apartment building. His face was covered in radiation burns, but he had consistently refused medical evaluation for radiation over-exposure. More information on Hahn can be found in Ken Silverstein's book The Radioactive Boy Scout.

Marie Curie (1867-1934, born Maria Sklodowska in Poland) was one of the earliest pioneers in the field of radioactivity, a term she herself coined. She developed some of the first theories of radioactivity, discovered and isolated the elements Polonium (named for her home country of Poland) and Radium, and pioneered the use of radiotherapy to treat cancer. She was awarded the 1903 Nobel Prize in Physics which was shared with her husband Pierre Curie and radioactivity co-discoverer Henri Becquerel, and the 1913 prize in Chemistry. She died in 1934 of Leukemia resulting from over-exposure to radiation. Pierre Curie died in 1906, run over by a horse-drawn cart. To this day, the Curies' notebooks are dangerously radioactive and must be stored in lead boxes.

Radium (atomic number 88) is one of the most radioactive elements found in nature. It is very rare, with only a seventh of a gram occurring per ton of Uranium ore. Following its discovery in1898, Radium was used for a wide variety of purposes. Encased in steel 'seeds', it was used in Brachytherapy, the treatment of cancer via direct implantation of radioisotopes into tumours. Mixed with a phosphor, Radium was also used as a self-illuminating paint for dials on clocks and aircraft instruments. These dials were often painted by young women in factories, who were not informed of Radium's adverse health effects. The women would often sharpen their brushes by licking them, and even playfully painted their nails and teeth. As a result, many died of bone cancer. The plight of the Radium Girls lead to the implementation of some of the first Occupational Health and Safety laws in the U.S. Today, less-dangerous Tritium gas is used for self-powered lighting (such as in gunsights).

The Downwinders

Between 1952 and 1963, Great Britain conducted 12 nuclear weapons tests in Australia. The first British atomic bomb, code-named Hurricane, was detonated on October 3, 1952 off the Montebello islands in the northwest of the continent. The 25 kiloton device was detonated in the hull of the frigate HMS Plym to simulate the effects of a ship-smuggled bomb. This was followed in 1952 by two tests codenamed Operation Totem, conducted at the temporary Emu Field site in Southern Australia. Two more tests (Operation Mosaic) were conducted in the Montebellos in 1956, before a permanent testing site was established at Maralinga, South Australia. Seven tests were conducted at Maralinga as part of Operations Buffalo and Antler. In 1957, the first British hydrogen bombs were tested near Christmas Island in the South Pacific (Operation Grapple). After the signing of the Limited Test Ban Treaty in 1963 (which forbade all atmospheric tests), all British nuclear tests were conducted underground at the Nevada Test Site in the U.S. The last British test, Julin Bristol, was conducted in 1991.

Much controversy surrounds the British nuclear testing programme in Australia, particularly in regards to fallout and the extent to which the Australian public was informed of potential dangers. During the Mosaic G2 test in 1956, prevailing winds carried the fallout cloud over Northern Australia rather than out to sea as intended. The government did not inform the public. Several days later, however, Luke van Houdt, a technician repairing Geiger counters the Air Force, discovered that the rain in Brisbane was highly radioactive. The tests at Emu Field and Maralinga also heavily contaminated surrounding areas. In particular, one of the Vixen B tests, meant to determine the effects of fire and explosions on nuclear weapons (as in the case of a nuclear bomber crash), sprayed 22 kilograms of highly-toxic Plutonium into the atmosphere. A perfunctory cleanup (Operation Brumby) was conducted in 1967, wherein contaminated soil was tilled under and other radioactive waste collected in concrete containers. This effort proved inadequate when, in subsequent years, locals began suffering radiation poisoning and increased cancer rates.

In 1985, the McClelland Royal Commission was convened to investigate the British Government's conduct regarding the nuclear tests. The commission found that many test sites were still heavily contaminated, and that large quantities of radioactive waste had simply been dumped into the sea off West Australia. They also found that many tests were conducted on traditional Aborigine land and that inadequate measures were taken to evacuate the native population. Hundreds of Aborigines died after being caught in the fallout cloud of the Totem-1 test. Australian soldiers were also ordered to march and crawl across contaminated ground as part of nuclear warfare exercises. The Australian Government eventually provided compensation for displaced Aborigines and veterans suffering from certain cancers. A $108 million cleanup was conducted from 1996 - 2000, though many sites remain heavily contaminated.

Recently declassified documents reveal that the Commonwealth Scientific and Industrial Research Organization (CSIRO) had, in secret, conducted a massive study to monitor the accumulation of radioisotopes in the bodies of Australian people. Over 20 years, bones from over 21,000 bodies—most of them children —were reduced to ash and tested for Strontium-90. The study revealed that Strontium-90 had contaminated the Australian milk supply via cows grazing on fallout-contaminated pasture.

The Curie is a measure of radioactivity, equivalent to 37 Billion becquerels (nuclear disintegrations per second). Absorbed radiation dose is measured in grays, equivalent to one joule of energy absorbed by one kilogram of matter. Similar units include the rad (one erg per gram), the sievert (one gray, calibrated for biological tissue), the roentgen (2.58x10-4 Coulombs electric charge per kilogram) and the rem (one roentgen, calibrated for biological tissue). The average person receives ~620 millirem of radiation per year.

A is for Atom

For those readers who may doubt that people such as Anne Mulligan exist, my personal experience suggests that they do. This story was inspired by a breakdown in relations between myself and a former friend—a breakdown sparked by ignorance of nuclear science. This friend and I were on very good terms and had many interests in common. Shortly after the Fukushima disaster in 2011, I happened to mention to a friend that I was a strong proponent of nuclear power. At this my friend became very angry, accusing me of the utmost arrogance, hubris and reckless contempt for the safety of humanity. Accepting no defense of the nuclear industry, she never spoke to me again. Her fiery reaction and views became the basis for the Anne Mulligan character.

All statistics quoted in this story (such as the quantity of radioactive waste in North America) are accurate as of this writing. More radiation is indeed absorbed by the average individual from airborne ash produced by coal-burning power plants and from radioactive Potassium in bananas. Indeed, the Banana Equivalent Dose (BED) is sometimes used in the nuclear industry as a measure of radiation exposure. Since the time of this writing, however, the proposed Yucca Mountain National Repository in Nevada has been cancelled. Both the United States and Canada are still without a permanent safe storage facility for radioactive waste.

The Highest Step

This story is based on the real-life Project Excelsior, a U.S. Air Force program which culminated in the highest skydive in history. In the late 1950s, as high-performance jet aircraft flew ever higher and faster, aircrew forced to eject at high altitudes faced new, unforeseen dangers. In the thin upper atmosphere, parachutes could fail to deploy properly and become tangled around the pilot. Tests with dummies dropped from high altitude also revealed that, unstablized, a pilot's body would enter a violent and potentially fatal spin. To avoid this, a pilot first had to deploy a small drogue chute, stabilizing his descent until he reached air sufficiently dense to deploy his main canopy. This was not possible, however, if a pilot was unconscious or otherwise incapacitated. In response, Air Force technician Francis Beaupré invented a multi-stage parachute with pressure sensors that would automatically deploy the drogue and main chutes at the correct altitudes, regardless of the pilot's condition. Project Excelsior (Latin for 'ever higher') began in 1958 to test Beaupré's invention.

The parachute system was tested using a 60-meter helium balloon, which could carry a test pilot in an open gondola to an altitude of over 5,000 meters. The test director for Excelsior was US Air Force Captain Joseph Kittinger, who had already broken several high-altitude ballooning records as part of Project Manhigh (1957). To survive the near vacuum and extremely low temperatures of the upper stratosphere, Kittinger wore a full pressure suit. Automatic cameras on the gondola—and on Kittinger's helmet—would capture his record-breaking jump.

The first jump, Excelsior I, nearly ended in disaster. On November 16, 1959, Kittinger jumped from an altitude of 23,287 meters over the New Mexico desert. The drogue chute opened too early, however, and wrapped itself around Kittinger's neck, sending him into a flat spin. Kittinger lost consciousness, but was saved when main parachute automatically deployed, just as designed. Despite this incident, Kittinger made a second attempt—Excelsior II—just three weeks later, jumping from 22,769 meters. This time everything went smoothly; the Beaupré parachute functioning perfectly.

Excelsior III, Kittinger's third and final jump, was made on August 16, 1960. Riding the gondola to 31,333 meters, he broke the previous altitude record set by Project Manhigh in 1957. During the hour-and-a-half ascent, the seal in Kittinger's right glove failed, exposing his hand to the vacuum. Despite experiencing severe pain and temporarily losing the use of his hand, Kittinger did not report the incident lest the flight surgeons abort the jump. At altitude, with 90% of the atmosphere below him, Kittinger activated his automatic cameras and calmly stepped out of the gondola. Trailing the stabilizing drogue, Kittinger fell for 4 minutes and 36 seconds before his main chute deployed. During this time he reached a speed of 998 km/hr, nearly breaking the speed of sound. 13 minutes and 45 seconds after jumping, Kittinger reached the ground. He had simultaneously broken the record for longest free-fall, highest parachute jump and fastest speed attained without a vehicle.

Kittinger's record was not broken until 52 years later, by Austrian skydiver Felix Baumgartner on October 14, 2012. As part of the Red Bull Stratos project, Baumgartner jumped from a helium balloon at an altitude of 39,045m (128,100 ft) and reached a maximum speed of 1,342.1 km/hr (833.9 mph) or Mach 1.24, making him the first human to break the sound barrier without a parachute. He also claimed the record for the highest manned balloon flight. During the jump, Baumgartner's Capsule Communicator (CapCom), the only person allowed to contact him by radio, was Joseph Kittinger.

The imagery in this story is based on Kittinger's recollections and original footage of the jumps. During the record-breaking Excelsior III jump, a placard was affixed to Kittinger's gondola, bearing the words: 'This is the Highest Step in the World'.

In the Ocean of Storms

Following President John F. Kennedy's 1960 announcement that the United States would be sending men to the moon by the close of the decade, the USSR initiated its own manned lunar project.

The Soviet moonshot was considerably different from Apollo Program in many respects. As the Russian lunar rocket, the N1, had only 70% the power of the American Saturn V, the spacecrafts it carried were considerably smaller and more stripped-down than their NASA counterparts. Following a mission profile similar to Apollo's Lunar-Orbit-Rendezvous, the N1 would have carried a modified Soyuz 7K-LOK capsule, an LK lunar landing craft and two cosmonauts into lunar orbit. As the LK had no crew transfer tunnel like the Apollo Lunar Module (LM), one cosmonaut would have to spacewalk from the Soyuz to the LK before undocking and beginning his lunar descent. A Blok D rocket stage would de-orbit the LK and send it hurtling towards the moon. Sent to the moon ahead of the cosmonauts would be an empty Soyuz capsule (for use as an emergency 'lifeboat') and a Lunokhod robotic rover, whose beacon would guide the LK to a precision landing. Once on the lunar surface, the lone cosmonaut would plant the flag, set up a handful of scientific experiments, and collect rock samples before re-entering the LK and lifting off. The landing legs would remain on the lunar surface, acting as a launch pad for the ascent stage. Unlike the American LM, which had separate ascent and descent engines, the LK used one engine for both tasks; if it failed, the cosmonaut would be stranded. Once back in lunar orbit, the cosmonaut would once again spacewalk back to the Soyuz before they discarded the LK and headed back to earth.

Two groups of flight crews were assembled for the projected lunar missions, which included such famous cosmonauts as Yuri Gagarin (the first man in space) and Aleksey Leonov, (the first man to perform an extravehicular activity (EVA) or 'spacewalk'). In 1967, however, disaster struck during Soyuz I, the first test flight of the lunar capsule. The mission, plagued by endless technical problems, ended with the death of cosmonaut Vladimir Komarov when his parachute failed to deploy after reentry. He was the first person in history to die on a space mission. After the disaster, Aleksey Leonov was seen as the likeliest candidate for the first cosmonaut to walk on the moon.

Typical of the Soviet space program as a whole, the Lunar project was constantly beset by rushed designs, technical failures, lack of funds, shifting political priorities and stifling bureaucracy. While the LK lander was successfully tested in earth orbit, it never made it to the moon—the N1 rocket that was to carry it failed on all four test-launch attempts. With the successful lunar landing of Apollo 11 on July 20, 1969, the raison d'etre of the Soviet manned lunar project evaporated and the program was soon cancelled. The project's very existence was kept a secret until the fall of the Soviet Union in 1991. Rather than admit they had lost the Space Race, the Soviets claimed that the United States had spent billions on a contest that never existed.

The Sky is Calling

The NASA Great Moonbuggy Race, started in 1993, is held annually at the Marshall Spaceflight Centre (MSC) in Huntsville, Alabama. The event, which attracts university and high school teams from around the world, challenges competitors to build 'moon buggies' in the same mould as the Lunar Roving Vehicle (LRV) used in the Apollo 15, 16, and 17 missions. Though the competition rovers must be human-powered (no motors, springs or other stored-energy devices are allowed), they must conform to design specifications comparable to the real LRV: every entry must be light enough for the two riders (one male, one female) to carry, must include mockups of antennae, batteries and other essential equipment, must fold to fit inside of a 4'x4'x4' cube (simulating storage space aboard the Lunar Module), and must be deployable from the folded position within a certain time limit. Qualifying entrants drive a timed circuit around a gravel track winding through the MSC's rocket park, which simulates lunar terrain including rilles and craters. The rover with the fastest lap wins.

The events in this story actually happened during my trip to the Great Moonbuggy Race in April 2010. One arduous day's driving after our fireworks adventure we arrived home, exhausted and bleary-eyed—just in time for final exams.

Epigraph sources

Lyon Sprague de Camp: American Author, 1907-2000
Louis Dudek: Canadian Poet, 1918-2001
Herbert George (H.G.) Wells: English Author, 1866-1946

Jean Cocteau: French Author, 1889-1963
Erwin Rommel: German Army General and Field Marshall, 1891-1944
William Hervey Allen: American Author 1889-1949

Julius Robert Oppenheimer: American Physicist, 1904-1967

Hippocrates: Greek physician and father of modern medicine, c.470-360 B.C.

Charles de Gaulle: French Army General and Statesman, 1890-1970

Freeman Dyson: English/American Physicist, 1923-
Richard Feynman: American Physicist, 1918-1988
Albert Einstein: German Physicist, 1979-1955

From A Thousand and One Nights

Herman Kahn: American futurist and military strategist, 1922-1983

Marie Curie (Maria Sklodowska): Polish/French Physicist & Chemist, 1867-1934

Wernher von Braun: German engineer, 1912-1977
Jim Lovell: American astronaut, 1928-
Konstantin Tsiolkovsky: Russian astronautics pioneer, 1857-1935

Francis Reginald Scott: Canadian Poet, 1899-1985

Valentina Tereshkova: Russian cosmonaut, 1937-

David Gilmour: English musician, 1946-

Control room of Battersea Power Station, London, July 1933. (right detail)
nickelinthemachine.com/2009/05/the-cathedral-of-electrons-in-battersea/

"Technology...is not mere set-dressing in the grand drama of humanity. It is humanity—its very soul and essence."
— *from the Author's preface*

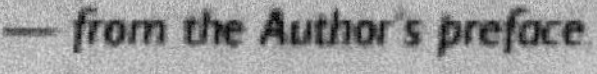

Mid-century speculative fiction

The Second World War. Nuclear Power. Space Exploration. Three powerful forces that forever changed the course of history. In these nine new stories based on historical fact, Gilles Messier explores our intimate and often fickle relationship with science and technology in the 1940s, 1950s and 1960s, and how it came to define our past, present and future.

Gilles Messier was born in Winnipeg in 1989 and studies aerospace engineering at Carleton University, Ottawa. As well as writing, he designs and develops mechanical devices and innovations. He enjoys painting 1930s-style travel posters, and studying history and philosophy.

Self-portrait, 2010

978-1-927032-06-0 (paperback edition)
978-1-927032-08-4 (smashwords edition)
2013

petrabooks.ca

ISBN 978-1-927032-06-0
90000
9 781927 032060